BLAZE IS DEMANDING. UNYIELDING.
A PUNISHER

He thinks he can rid me of my demons
by exacting even more of me than I ask of myself.
He says he can wash my sins clean.
Absolve me of the fire that scalded my soul.
All I have to do is turn myself over to him.
Submit. Surrender.
The only problem—he doesn't just want my body.
He wants to own my life.

Note: This steamy romance contains a dominant, dirty talking
fireman, a fiery new recruit and enough kink to start a three-alarm
fire. If such material offends you, please do not read this book!

WANT FREE RENEE ROSE BOOKS?

Click here to sign up for Renee Rose's newsletter and receive a free copy of *Theirs to Protect, Owned by the Marine, Theirs to Punish, The Alpha's Punishment, Disobedience at the Dressmaker's* and *Her Billionaire Boss*. In addition to the free stories, you will also get special pricing, exclusive previews and news of new releases.

AUTHOR'S NOTE

Thank you so much for reading my firefighter romance. If you enjoyed it, I would so appreciate your review—they make a huge difference for indie authors.

My enormous gratitude to Aubrey Cara and Maura Pritchard for their beta reads and for Maggie Ryan's editing. I love you guys!

Thanks also to the amazing members of my Facebook group, Renee's Romper Room. The kink talk and support inspire me every day!

CHAPTER 1

 ia

WITH FOUR BROTHERS—ALL cops, not firemen—I'm not afraid of any guy. Especially not guys like these.

Even if their, I mean *our*, captain doesn't want a female on the crew.

"What are you playing?" I ask my new teammates innocently as they deal another round of poker to kill time at the station.

Rocket—the friendliest, but possibly dorkiest—grins. "Poker—know how to play?"

I twirl the end of my dark ponytail around my finger. "Yeah, I think so."

James, who is the least friendly of the guys—not counting the captain—folds his arms over his large chest. "We don't play for money, though."

I know what's coming and I'm not afraid. "Oh yeah?" I'm pretty good at playing innocent. "What do you play for?"

"Have you heard of strip poker?"

Rocket flushes slightly, clearly thrilled by the suggestion. "Yeah, it's just for fun," he leers. "That way if we get a call, the person who took off the most takes the longest to get ready."

Uh huh. *Right.*

I pull a chair up to the table. "Okay. I'm in."

"You are?" Rocket's eyes pop, like he can't believe how lucky they got.

James still looks like he tasted a lemon, but he starts shuffling and deals the cards.

I sit back, hold my cards and hide my inner smirk. If these asshole firemen believe they can haze me into taking my clothes off and becoming their wet dream fire maiden, I'll let them harbor that impossible fantasy—for at least another half hour.

See—here's what I know. Firemen are nicer than cops. More predictable. They have that same hero desire but it burns—*heh*—brighter. They're not quite as power-hungry or controlling. Except for the captain. They call him Blaze—I'm guessing because of a temper. He's got a streak of controlling cop for sure. It's a trait that I hate in my brothers, but unfortunately makes my knees go weak in a boss. Especially a fire captain boss.

The rest of these boys were the football stars in high school—good-looking, rigid thinkers, slightly chauvinistic, but generally nice guys. No one's gonna actually get naked here and they know it. Oh, they probably think they're gonna get an eyeful of my bra and panties, maybe even harbor hope of seeing some boobage—not that there's much to see—but they don't know who they're up against.

If anyone knows how to play poker, it's me.

Again—four brothers.

What my brothers don't know is that I also know how to play

dingy sex kitten and make stupid would-be poker champs think I'm in over my head.

Which means, at the end of *this* game, these boys are going to be the ones sitting in their boxer briefs, and I'm going to be using my phone to take pictures I can forever hold over their heads.

"So, Lia," Scott, my thirty-something hot but ignorant new colleague drawls, "It's you."

"We need a better name for her," Rocket says.

"Yeah, too bad Rocket's already taken," I say drily.

He grins good-naturedly. "How about Sparks? She's definitely a little spark plug, plus she's always lighting matches."

Damn, they noticed that. I just burned a few outside between fires to let off steam. I'll have to be more careful.

"It's your bet, Sparks," James says without a smile. "Let me guess, you're starting with your boots."

"Nope." I make a show of slowly peeling my red FDNY t-shirt over my head. "I'll open." All three of the other firefighters on duty tonight stare. "Let's start with the shirt. That way you guys can get a nice look at what's *not* coming off tonight." I squeeze both my breasts through the very chaste, full-coverage pink sports bra.

Scott's hand drops under the table, presumably to rearrange his junk. "I see." He clears his throat. "Didn't expect that from you."

I hide my triumph. They thought they'd force me to admit I can't claim to be just one of the guys. Cock-teasing is my surprise rebuttal.

He, too, peels his shirt off, revealing a perfect pair of pects on a gleaming dark-skinned chest. Not that I'm looking. Every guy here is ripped. Being physically fit is part of the job requirement. But I'm used to guys like these from the CrossFit gym. "I'll see your shirt." He stands up and unbuttons his Nomex pants. "And raise you a pair of pants."

"Ooh," James and Rocket croon, looking for my reaction.

I can't hold back my smirk. If they think showing me their

3

boxers is going to fluster me, they have a shit-ton of more thinks coming. I can give it as well as they do.

I completed my fire training. I worked three summers as a hot-shot for the Forest Service in Arizona. No female is in better shape than I am right now. And still I had to apply and reapply for thirty-two months to get this job. No one will say it, but I guarantee it's about their bias against my small size and gender.

But I'm putting that behind me because I finally landed this job —despite the intimidating interview with the chief and battalion chief. And now that I got it, I'm going to prove how well I fit in. There won't be awkwardness. They'll respect me as much as they do anyone else.

"What. *The fuck*. Is going on here?"

At the sound of the captain's angry boom, we all jump and throw our cards down, sitting up straight.

This is how I know deep down these are nice boys. They have the grace to go completely shame-faced, hurriedly scooping up the cards and tossing me my shirt.

"Nothing, Captain," Scott says, yanking his own shirt back on.

Our hard-assed captain, Ted MacKenzie—Blaze—is like the Greek god of firemen. Tall, tattooed and beef-alicious, he's young to be in charge—maybe in his mid-thirties. And what he lacks in years he makes up for in gruffness. The man is two hundred fifty pounds of pure authority and alpha male dominance. A fact I find far too sexy for my own good.

And he definitely isn't happy right now. Laser beams shoot from his striking blue eyes. Anger radiates from him, letting us all know we're in deep shit.

"Aw, we're just indoctrinating Sparks into our poker games, Cap," Rocket says.

"Sparks, huh." His eyes shoot to me and he flicks his brows. "Fitting."

I square my shoulders to hide the fact that I'm cowed. And

turned on. My pussy clenches and damn my nipples—they prod the inside of my sports bra. But I'm like this in Blaze's presence all the time. I'm always attracted to the guys who don't think I'm good enough.

What does that say about me?

And since this guy seemed pissed as hell to be assigned a female to his crew, I suddenly question the wisdom of our little strip poker game. He looks ready to commit murder. We each receive our own special glare, which travels slowly around the circle until we're all sweating like kids sent to the principal's office.

"This is not a goddamn frat house. Burke is here to work, like the rest of you. She's not here for you to stroke your pathetic dicks. You're going to treat her like any other goddamn fireman—fireperson—*whatever.*" He throws up an impatient hand. He jerks his chin at me. "Put your shirt on."

My cheeks flame, but I hold his gaze with a note of defiance as I slide it on.

No matter—he's back to lecturing the guys, pointing his finger at each one in turn. "We haven't had a woman on the crew before, but that doesn't mean you lose your goddamn heads. I expect every one of you to figure out how to be appropriate starting today. Right now." He points at the ground. "You don't make suggestive remarks, you don't talk about sex around her and you *sure as hell don't try to get her to do a goddamn strip tease.* If I ever see this kind of shit again, I will write you up on harassment so fast your heads will spin. *Is that perfectly clear?*"

"Yes, sir," they all say immediately.

"And God help any of you if I ever hear you try anything with her. You will lose more than your job, you will lose your nuts."

The guys, who had been sitting up straight for the brutal lecture, sink down in their seats.

"This firehouse is a strict no-fraternizing zone." He looks at me for that.

I had been slightly flattered by the protective note to his lecture, but now white hot anger pours through me. I stick my chin out but somehow manage to keep my mouth shut.

But seriously? Is he implying I'm trying to seduce my co-workers? What a prick.

He keeps the blazing gaze fixed on me. "And you. You worked your ass off to get into this firehouse. Don't fuck it up now." He turns and walks away.

I'm on my feet—definitely too pissed to be around these guys a minute longer. I stalk to the tiny cubicle that serves as my bedroom for the night and shut the door, reaching for a book of matches with shaking hands.

The scrape of the head and bright flare of the flame calm me. The sulfur stings my nostrils and sends the signal to my brain. Like an addict getting a hit, my body responds. My muscles relax, heart rate slows. My pleasure centers activate.

I hold the match, letting it burn down to my fingers before I drop it in the metal wastebasket. I'm safe with matches. If anyone knows the danger of fire, it's me. I light another, then one more until I've soothed the tiger.

I flick another match. Damn the prickly captain for screwing up what would've been a perfectly genial way to break the boys in. I drop the match in the trash can. Damn the prickly captain for making me want to prove myself to him all over again. I drop the matches on the desk and stand up. Fuck it. I *am* going to give him a piece of my mind.

～

Blaze

I'm all about equal rights—I am.

But having Lia Burke in my firehouse might be the death of me.

I head back to the station office and sit at the desk. Lord. I can't fucking believe they sent me a tiny female. Sure, she passed the test. She's strong and looks tough as hell. Definitely one of those CrossFit chicks who can bench twice her weight.

But her presence here is going to be the biggest pain in my ass ever.

She's also *hot*. Her smooth caramel skin looks downright lickable, and the big green eyes are set off by long, curling lashes. Not the fake kind that are so popular these days. Natural lashes—no mascara or anything, not that I'm an expert on these things.

And she has junk in the trunk. I'm definitely an ass man and this girl? She has the best posterior I've ever had the pleasure of walking behind. Not that I do that on purpose.

Not unless I want to sprout wood in front of my crew.

I can't stand the other guys ogling her. I mean, I seriously can't stand it.

They are not exactly PC. It's locker room talk around here twenty-four seven. I swear I'm going to have a sexual harassment claim on my hands in less than a month.

Even though she's trying to prove she's cool with whatever they throw her way.

Yeah, the little spitfire is going to turn this firehouse on its head.

But what troubles me even more is I know something about this girl.

I started at the Staten Island station—Ladder 153. There was a three-alarm fire that destroyed a cop's place ten years ago. The cop's oldest son was friends with our captain—my buddy who is now a battalion chief. When Lia got hired, he reminded me of a fire we put out.

We tried so hard to save the house, but it was too late—the entire thing was made of sticks and went up fast. I remember the

Puerto Rican wife crying in Spanish while the cop and his kids tried to be heroes and help. We had to order back the four boys and one girl a number of times.

The fire had been ruled accidental, originating in the girl's bedroom. That girl was Lia Burke.

And for some reason, knowing her history makes me even more protective of her.

She's fighting demons. She became a firefighter to try reverse her past.

As if that ever works. We can't make up for our past mistakes. I should know.

A prickle on the back of my neck tells me I'm being watched and I look up. Here she is—one hip propped against my doorway, her slender but buff arms folded across her chest.

She's so small we had to order her a child's size t-shirt for her to wear, but damn, the spunk in her is anything but petite. Her dark curls are pulled up in a high ponytail, dark-lashed green eyes are bright against her flushed skin.

"Yes, Burke?" I have to work hard not to think about the way her nipples got hard when I was going off on the crew.

Damn.

I work even harder not to wonder what that means.

Her jaw muscles tighten, then release, then tighten again.

Little girl is trying to hold her tongue and, if I'm interpreting correctly, not blow up at me. I *really* have to work to force back all the fantasies that crowd my brain about punishing her for sass. Or forcing her to speak her mind. It could easily go either way.

Another beat passes and she pushes her hip off the door frame. "Nevermind." She turns and walks away, the sway of her perky ass making my cock twitch in my pants.

"No, come back. Let's talk this out. You pissed at me?" I may be a hardass, but I'm actually all about communication amongst the team.

When she turns, her expression's softened, relief flickering over it. She leans a hand against the doorframe, staying outside it. "Kinda. Were you implying I was trying to—"

I hold my hands up. "I wasn't implying anything." I stand up from the chair. I'm a big guy, and she's freakin' tiny, but she doesn't draw back. If anything, she leans forward, eyes dilating. "Strip poker isn't allowed in this firehouse under my watch, that's it. End of story."

Her mouth turns down at the corners.

"Listen, you're trying to find your place here—getting to know the guys. I get it." I shove my hands in my pockets to seem less threatening. "I'm sure you would've had them all in their boxer shorts by the time you were done."

A smile quirks before she hides it again, her body posture relaxing even more. I like putting her at ease. Almost as much as I liked seeing her reaction—physical, anyway—to my dominance back there.

"The thing is—we haven't had a woman on the team before. It's going to be an adjustment for all of us. And I don't want anyone thinking..."

I stop because, what am I going to say? I don't want them thinking the same thing I am about her? How much they'd love to feel that tight little body squirming underneath theirs? How they'd love to give her a little *personal* training?

"I don't want anyone to fuck with you, that's all. Because then I'd have to pound their faces in."

This time I succeed in wringing a real grin from her—one that stays on her face and makes her big eyes crinkle. She's unbelievably pretty, with flawless skin and a pair of dimples. It takes all my willpower not to drop my gaze to her breasts, because I'm dying to see if I made those little nipples hard again.

She rolls her eyes. "So you're playing big brother, not boss? I already have four of those, so it's not really a role I need filled."

Oh, sugar, my thoughts are anything but brotherly.

"Yeah—I'm Big Brother with the capital Bs. Always watching." I do the two fingers at my eyes, two fingers at her eyes gesture and she laughs. Something that buckled down across my chest when I walked in on the guys' shenanigans releases. "I see you can take care of yourself, Sparks. Just don't make me sorry you got placed here."

"Okay, there it is." She's fully in my office now, hands on her hips. "I knew there was something you were trying to say to me. So what is it?"

Her show of defiance makes my cock ache. I want to take this girl in hand so badly my palm twitches. I can't stop myself from advancing on her until we're toe to toe. Nose to chest.

I'm dying to wrap my fist in her hair, tip that saucy head back to keep her eyes on my face. Fortunately for her, she lifts them of her own accord.

"Enough, little dragon." I tower over her, hands on my hips. "You don't march into my office breathing fire and throwing out attitude. You have something to say to me, you show some respect."

She swallows and takes a step back. "I'm sorry, sir."

Christ, yes. The nipples are hard. Even through a sports bra and t-shirt. Her eyes are dilated, too, and the way she rubs her lips together makes my cock chubby.

"That's better." I pin her with an authoritative stare and let the silence stretch between us before I go on. "I didn't say anything to you I wouldn't have said if you were a man."

She rolls her tongue around in her cheek. "You call the other guys *little dragon?*"

I fight a smile. "Did that offend you?"

She cocks a hip, her posture turned seductive. "Nah."

"Good. Are we okay?" I automatically reach out to thump her shoulder the way I would one of the guys after a talk in the office.

At the last second, I pull the thump part back and just touch her. It's just a shoulder—it's not like I have hands on her face, or her waist, or anywhere intimate—and yet it's like time freezes the moment I touch her. Our eyes lock, heat races through my limbs. I have to force myself to drop my hand but when I do, my gaze falls on those full, pouty lips.

Damn.

"Yeah, we're good." She's lost most of her tough girl attitude, her expression more wondering now. It's amazing how badly I want to see her stripped bare to me—the facade gone. I want to know the real Lia—what makes her tick.

But that won't be happening. No stripping—of clothes or otherwise. Not for me or any other asshole in this station.

CHAPTER 2

ia

I HOP off the Staten Island Railway a couple blocks from my parents' place and hoof it over, a pan of triple chocolate brownies in hand. It's my nephew's birthday, which means the entire house will be packed with family—my brothers and their wives and children, parents, uncles, aunts and then any neighbors who feel like stopping by and enduring the mayhem of the Burke family.

I know I'm not always up for it, that's for damn sure. Still, there's comfort in the known. The predictability of how the afternoon will play out. Every annoying comment has already been said before.

Of course, this is the first time I've seen everyone since I got the job at the fire station, so I have to brace myself for the millions of questions that will entail. I look up at the house, rebuilt to look exactly the same after the fire destroyed everything ten years ago. Given the chance for something new, my mom chose the known. Like her life could only be imagined one way and anything different would be wrong.

Me—I never wanted to come back here. Certainly not after the fire. Not now after being on my own for five years. I took off the second I graduated high school to 'find myself.' But I'm used to the familiar ache in my chest at returning. The heaviness of being back with everything so familiar and foreign at once.

Three of the older children bang out the door and race down the steps, laughing like they're up to no good. Which I fully applaud.

I step inside. "Hey, everyone!" I call out.

"Lia! Whatcha got there?" My Uncle Juan—my mother's brother—peers into my pan and snags a chunk of brownie where it crumbled up when I cut it. "Mmm." He pops it into his mouth. "That's a winner."

I twist to hold the pan out of his reach and walk past him to the kitchen toward the long table packed with every other dish of party food brought by the masses. Like my crazy family, a combination of Puerto Rican—my mom's side, and Irish—my dad's, favorites. Plates heaped with fried plantains, sliced jicama with lime squeezed over it, cilantro rice and beans, plus the platter of barbequed meat—hamburgers, hot dogs, bratwurst, Italian sausage. Packages of buns riddle the table, along with every condiment known to man.

I plunk the brownies down as my brother, Tommy, sweeps by and grabs a handful of chips. "There's the little traitor."

They like to rib me for joining the fire department instead of the police force. As if they ever would've let me follow them into the profession. I give him a hug and kiss my niece, Madison, the cherubic three-year-old perched on his hip. She kicks to be let down and runs off to join the rest of the kids.

My mom gets me next, with the two-cheeked kisses and a stream of chatter I don't even hear. I have this automatic tune-out that happens when I'm here. I'm so used to being talked over, unheard, projected on, that I just sort of settle into the hologram of what they see me as. I swear, until the day I packed up to join the Forest Service summer hotshot crew, no one comprehended I really intended to pursue my ambition to become a firefighter.

I still don't think anyone believes I can do it.

"Hey, squirt." My brother Eddie wraps an arm around me from behind, picks me off my feet and gives me a shake. "Yep. Still tiny."

"Small in size, not in personality," I sing. Again, this is routine. I could do it in my sleep.

"Hey, there she is!" My dad gives me a kiss. "You giving them hell over there?"

"Yep, Dad. All good." I pat his shoulder. Don't need Dad or my brothers to go apeshit protective on me. Because Lord knows, they would.

He shakes his head. "I still don't like the idea of you—"

I hold up my hand. "Yeah, yeah, yeah. I know—way too dangerous for your little girl. I can take care of myself, Dad."

My father looks genuinely pained and I experience a moment of remorse. I'm sure he does worry about me. And it's true this job is dangerous. But no more or less dangerous than being a cop, which was fine for all of my brothers.

It's the curse of being the youngest, a girl, and the only one in the family who got my mother's height. It's like they will forever think I'm still that little girl running around in footed pajamas or something.

All he says is, "I sure hope so, sweetheart," and ambles on.

I fix myself a plate of food and head outside to the back, where more meat is being grilled by the man-pack gathered around. This is where I feel like I don't belong. I've always had that sense. The women here are all talking about the children, and families and stuff that doesn't interest me. Before there were nieces and nephews, they were talking about girl shit that didn't interest me. I can fake it, but I always have that sense I'm a stranger in my own family. I open a folding chair and plunk myself down on it.

My oldest brother, Alex, sets up a chair beside me. "So?"

"So, what?"

"The guys hazing you?"

I roll my eyes. "That's what Dad asked, too. Are you going to go kick their asses if I say they are?"

"Hell yeah, I'm going to kick their asses! Nobody messes with my baby sister."

I bump shoulders with him and stand up. "I can take care of myself."

"Wait up, Lia." I turn back. "I got a friend over there—not at your station, but he's a battalion chief. He told me they're taking bets on how long you'll last."

Seriously?

Even though I'd guessed this much, hearing it confirmed sends a flush of white hot anger and oily humiliation mixing in my veins. I suddenly hate the men I work with, and my brother for relaying this shit to me. I blink rapidly, my eyes and nose burning.

"Oh yeah?" I square my shoulders. "What are you betting?"

He holds his hands up. "Whoa, whoa. I'm on your side."

"Really? How is telling me that a help?" I snap. I've raised my voice, which gathers some attention from the family members around.

He pulls a long face and shoves his hands deep in his pockets. "I just thought you should know what you're up against."

"Yeah, I do know. Not that every member of this family hasn't warned me at least fifty times each."

I have a tendency to exaggerate. Sue me.

I turn on my heel and head into the house, ignoring Alex calling my name.

Inside my mom is talking to one of my sisters-in-law about some toy. "I had the same set of alphabet blocks my mother saved for me. All five kids played with them—long after they were little. It breaks my heart they were all lost in the fire."

My eyes dart to the burn scars on her forearm and my stomach clenches. I've heard this refrain so often over the last ten years but it never gets easier. The gnawing guilt never goes away.

And this is why I'm not giving up. I'm not going to be hazed into quitting.

I had to become a firefighter.

Because me and fire—we like each other way too much. And if there's anyone who should be running into burning buildings and pulling out kids, it's me.

I owe the world that much.

CHAPTER 3

 ia

THE ALARM SOUNDS through the fire station. My heart pumps as I rush through the steps that training ingrained into me. I pull on my turnouts and step into my boots, faster this time than the last three times. My time is improving.

I climb behind the wheel of our fire truck. There are five of us on the crew, and Blaze assigned me the chauffeur job. I know it's because he thinks I'm not strong enough for the other jobs. Like I didn't pass the same firefighter test all the rest of them did.

Which is fine. I'll show them all soon enough. I put on my earmuffs and start the engine and lights.

"Everyone in?" I'm ready to pull out when I hear a bang on the side of the truck.

"Hold up." The front passenger door swings open.

Terence, who is sitting shotgun with me, looks up in surprise.

"I'm riding up front." It's the captain.

Terence moves immediately and Blaze climbs in beside me.

Damn the man. He's keeping an eye on me.

I swear he's put himself next to me on every fire to make sure I can do the job. Or maybe he's trying to prove I can't.

Well, if he wants to intimidate me, I'm not going to scare so easily. That's what all these guys expect. I see the doubt on their faces. No one here thinks I can handle a serious fire. In fact, I wouldn't be surprised if hiring me was some kind of equal employment opportunity—or whatever it's called—some mandate to prove the FDNY isn't discriminating against females. In which case, my brother was right and this crew probably intends to haze me until I quit on my own.

So far, in the four tours I've worked since I started, the guys haven't welcomed me into their circle yet. Aside from our ill-fated poker game, I haven't been included in any socializing. Conversations die when I appear. It's been worse since the poker incident, like now they're gun-shy about joking with me. My attempts to fit in have failed. I know how guys shit each other. They're not acting normal around me.

But I'm going to make sure that, in addition to being capable of the job, I can hang with the worst of them.

"You worried I'm going to cry when I break a nail, Captain?" I challenge as I pull out into traffic, siren wailing.

His sensual lips tighten and a muscle ticks in his jaw. "Shut up and drive, Burke."

"Yes, sir, that's what I'm doing."

Blaze can be a dick, but that doesn't stop my raging attraction to him. Too bad I have to pick the guy who seems to want me here the least to drool over.

"Just making sure you can really handle yourself."

Well. At least I know where I stand. I tip my hard hat to him. "I appreciate the vote of confidence."

He surveys me with cool blue eyes, but says nothing.

Whatever.

Even my own family thinks I'm incapable of keeping this job. They never thought I'd land a position in the first place. When I did finally get hired, my mom cried. And they weren't tears of joy. If it wasn't for the constant encouragement from my cousin Talia, a journalist and environmental activist in Mapleton, a small town outside Chicago, I probably would've given up on this dream.

We pull up in front of an old brick building—a Catholic high school.

Arson fire. Set by a student. I don't know how I know, but I do. I know the mind of a teen pyro.

The flicker of flames light the windows on a lower wing. The captain directs me to the nearest fire hydrant and I line the truck up perfectly, then jump out and start my job of getting the pump in gear.

The captain stays on my ass, letting Scott do the officer-in-command thing, providing initial size-up and forcible entry. I set the pump to the right pressure and get the water flowing. We have the fire out in ninety-eight minutes. Damage reached the second floor, but the sturdy brick and concrete construction kept the building from sustaining structural problems.

I can't shake the urge to figure out where the fire started—to prove my hunch is correct.

A heavy hand claps down on my shoulder. "Good work, Sparks."

I turn, hoping it's the captain, but it's Scott.

I kick myself for wanting Blaze's approval so badly. I know I'm doing a good job and that's all that matters, right? So far, I haven't frozen up once. Even when I wanted to just stand back and watch the flames, my fascination with the destruction is a deadly pull. It must be that same pull that nudges me about this fire.

The guys are packing the hose back up, and I should be helping, but I slip away for a chance to do some searching on my own. I circle around to the back corner where the fire was biggest.

There, outside a broken window, I find a gasoline can.

"Burke!" the captain calls, jogging over to me. "Why the fuck aren't you helping pack up the truck?"

"I was just trying to figure out the cause of the fire." I point out the gasoline can.

He purses his lips. "Don't touch anything. We'll leave it for the inspector to investigate."

I nod.

"And Burke? You're not an inspector. If you wanted to search out clues, you shoulda been a cop like the rest of your family. Now get back with the team."

Asshole.

"Yes, sir."

But then I realize what he revealed. *He knows my family.* Why does that set off alarm bells? Is he the source of information for my brother's friend at another station? The one who told him they're betting on how long I last?

"I don't need a fucking hero, understand?"

"Yes, sir," I repeat.

I'm not trying to be a hero. I know that's why most of them are here, but not me. I'm here because I have twin needs that will never be quenched: Fire. And atonement.

Blaze

I SMELL the scent of sulfur from behind Lia's closed door and grit my teeth. She's lighting matches again. That girl seriously needs a talking to. I rap sharply on the door and push it open.

—and then I stop cold.

Or maybe *hot* is the right word.

Lia's standing there in a pair of goddamn pink panties, her FDNY t-shirt knotted above her waist.

I gape for one room-spinning moment, then I step in to shut the door. Wait—*fuck!* I can't be in a closed room with her—*when she's in her panties!*

But I sure as hell can't leave it open for other fire-fucks to see her this way, either.

Screw it—I kick it closed.

She's laughing at me now, triumph over my dance with the door evident in her eyes.

"What in the Sam-fuck are you wearing?" I boom, too loud.

Her full lips stretch into a shit-eating grin. She loves seeing my unfortunately full-bodied reaction to the sight of a mere triangle of soft pink fabric covering what must be the sweetest little pussy in the five boroughs. "I'm pretty sure you're aware of what I'm wearing."

"Th-those are not regulation," I sputter. What I mean is that they look like they're made of a non-compliant material—like polyester or a rayon blend. And yeah, I shouldn't be looking that close, but I did.

If we run out on a fire tonight and she gets burned, those panties would melt and fuse to her skin.

I force myself to look away. I can't discuss it with her standing there like that. My self-control will frazzle. "Just... stop playing with fire. Put your pants on."

"Why, Captain?" the little minx purrs, knowing she has me by the balls. She cocks a hip. "Am I making you... *uncomfortable?*"

My fingers twitch. "Put some goddamn pants on before I spank that juicy ass red!"

Oh shit.

I clap a hand over my mouth, then attempt to hide the gesture by rubbing the stubble on my face. I definitely shouldn't have said that. All this time I've been trying to protect her from harassment, and I'm the first asshole to bring it.

Well, I knew that, didn't I? In reality, I've just been trying to protect her from me.

Of course, I can't tear my gaze from her now, and I watch her eyes grow dark, full lips part. Her nipples bead up beneath the t-shirt. "Wow, Captain," her voice sounds breathy and high. She reaches one hand between her legs and curls her fingers in. "That's kinda hot. Maybe I should take them off for that." She hooks her thumbs in the waistband of her panties and starts to slowly pull them down.

"Stop it." I stride forward and catch her wrists. In about two seconds I have her backed against the wall, wrists pinioned in one of my hands.

She's not breathing. I guess I'm not either.

"Fuck," I curse. "I'm pretty sure you just lost me my job." Not that it makes me any more willing to let her go. Unless I see a real protest, I'm seeing this scene through, job be damned.

"No," she pants. Her eyes are huge, pupils blown. "No one's losing their job. No one's going to talk about this." She licks her lips. "What we're doing."

"What are we doing?" My voice is so deep I don't recognize it.

"Um…" She sways her hips. "Were you going to punish me?"

Victory flushes through me. I can't fucking believe it. I thought I saw the signs of interest—that authority turned her on—but to hear her actually say it…

Damn.

This girl can't be real.

I don't need any further encouragement. "Yeah, I am." I back up enough to spin her around and plant her two hands on the wall. "Push that ass out, baby. You've had this coming for a while now."

She's clearly not afraid. She inches her feet away from the wall and hollows her back.

I bite back a groan.

The panties are tiny—satin and lace cutting across only half of her delicious ass. I gather the fabric up and thread it between her ass cheeks, pulling it taut against her clit and anus.

The little *oh!* she makes sends my already hard dick surging against my regulation pants.

I don't wait; I smack her ass cheek hard, right and left, two times each. "I came in here to talk about the goddamn matches." I deliver four more hard smacks. "And now we have to deal with your sass and these unauthorized—albeit cute—pink panties." I pull up tighter and smack her with a whole series of spanks, right and left, then the backs of her thighs.

Her hands drop and I think she's going to try to cover her ass—I'm already cursing myself for smacking too hard—but she brings one between her legs.

Christ! She's as turned on as I am.

By *spanking.*

It's like every wet dream of my teenage years just came true. And I'm about ready to blow my wad as fast as I did at fifteen, too.

"Uh uh." I grab her wrist and pin it back to the wall, delivering another flurry of spanks. "You don't get pleasure until I decide you get pleasure."

"Oh God," she moans. "I knew you'd be the guy."

I stop, intrigue shoving between the waves of lust, forcing me to slow down and gather more intel. "What guy?"

"Nevermind." She shakes her head, but her hair is pulled back in the ponytail, and I see the flush of pink tinge her cheeks.

Adorable.

I pick up spanking again—three hard ones. "Don't say *never-mind* to me, little girl. You're in no position not to answer my questions."

She moans like she's about to come, even though all I'm doing is smacking her ass and riding her clit with her underwear.

I work the panties, pulsing them up and releasing them like I'm fucking her with the fabric.

"Jesus, Maria y Jose!"

I laugh, because I haven't heard her speak even one word of Spanish before, and I didn't even know she could. "I've been told I have a god complex, but I don't think that's what you meant. What guy?"

She won't look away from the wall. "Spank me," she whispers.

Fuuuuuuuuck.

Now I don't want to. Now I just want to squeeze and massage her ass. Rub away the sting and reward her for being so damn good. As I do, she starts moaning. It's way too much for me.

I slip a hand around the front of her hips and rub her clit over the taut fabric of her panties. "You want to come, little dragon?"

"Yes, Daddy."

Oh, fuck. She did not just call me *daddy.*

I bite her shoulder, rock my throbbing cock against her ass. "Tell me what guy," I murmur in her ear.

"The one who does this," she croaks, snapping her hips like she's trying to push her cunt into my fingers.

That's it. I'm done for. I release her panties in the back and shove my fingers down the front, hooking them into her wet heat. I work my hand against her clit, and reposition myself to her side so I can slap her ass at the same time.

"Jesus, Blaze," she bites out, rising to her tiptoes, dancing over my hand in an attempt to take me deeper. She reaches one hand down on top of mine and presses against my fingers, while she rocks forward and back.

I smack her ass again, and again.

She squeals and comes, her pussy contracting around my fingers as she throws her head back against my chest. Her entire body convulses in sharp jerks and thrusts. It's the most beautiful thing I've ever seen.

~

Lia

OF ALL THINGS HOLY, I never dared dream Blaze would make this fantasy come true. I mean, he's featured in several lurid fantasies since I started here, but not this particular one.

My entire body is aflame, washed in hot tingles and warm pleasure.

And he's acting grateful, kissing and nipping my neck, holding me up because my legs are made of Jello. The bulge of his cock presses against my stinging ass.

I definitely want to return the favor. I extricate myself from his hold to turn around, then palm his erection through his pants.

His breath rasps in on a ragged inhale, and then he curses. "I don't have a condom."

I drop to my knees and unbutton his pants.

"Aw, Christ, Lia. You're blowing my mind right now."

Good. And I haven't even started. I pull his erection out of his boxers and grip the thick base. Lord, I'm not sure this will all fit in my mouth, and I never learned the trick of swallowing it down. Although for this guy, I'll try.

His belly shudders as I drag my tongue from balls to tip. I widen my lips and take him in, savoring the salty taste of his pre-cum. "This should not be happening," Blaze mutters, but he grasps the back of my head and pulls me forward over his cock.

His groan is all the encouragement I need. I suck hard, hollowing my cheeks as I pull slowly back.

An unintelligible syllable falls from Blaze's lips. It sounds ragged and pained.

That's right, big guy. I'll make you glad I got hired here.

I take him deep, bumping the back of my throat. I gag and pull back. Dammit. That was not how it's done.

"It's okay," Blaze soothes, running his thumb over my cheek far more gently than he holds the back of my head. I go for it again, taking it slower, forcing myself to relax the back of my throat.

I get it down!

"Fuck, baby. You're taking me so deep. Where'd you learn to suck like that... no don't tell me. I don't want to have to break any arms."

My laugh forces me off him, but he pulls me back on. "No, no, no, no. Don't stop now, little dragon. I need your hot little fire-breathing mouth around my cock so bad."

I believe him, because his thighs quake, balls bounce as they draw up tight.

I take him with fast pumps of my mouth, sending the head of his cock into the pocket of my cheek.

The alpha male in him resurfaces, and he grips both sides of my head, pumping me faster. Any other guy, I'd shove back or smack his hands away, but with Blaze? After what he just did? He can mouth fuck me all he wants, it just makes me wetter.

He growls. Chokes. Comes—hard. Hot streams of his essence shoot into my mouth. I close my eyes and force myself to swallow. Again, not one of my strong suits. I'm proud of myself when I manage it without wincing.

His hands gentle, fingers stroke my ears, cup my nape. When I pull off, he lifts me up and takes my mouth as he tucks his dick away. His kiss is every bit as dominating as the rest of his actions.

I don't know what I thought would happen next—some

awkward conversation about what we just did and how it can't happen again, maybe. I'm praying it's nothing drastic like him saying he has to transfer me.

It seems he's not done with whatever this was. He walks me backward to the cot and tips me onto my back, climbing on top of me.

"Okay, little dragon. We still have some talking to do." He pins my wrists beside my head and straddles my hips.

I've already come, but I'm so hot and ready to go again, I curse the fact that he doesn't have condoms.

"I came in here for a reason."

I struggle against his hold on my wrists, only because I want to feel his strength. "Oh yeah? What's that?" My voice comes out breathy and sweet. Not at all like my usual posturing.

"Did I smell matches in here?" He quirks a brow.

Part of me resists this conversation even though I knew it would come. Now that he's in here, pinning me to the bed, I have to wonder if I wasn't half hoping to someday be taken to task. If that's not the real reason I pursued this career. To end this dangerous addiction once and for all.

I blink up at his steely blue gaze, my insides warm and melty from the hot sex and his dominance. "Maybe."

He arches a brow. "Maybe? Or yes? Don't play coy with me unless you want another round with my hand and your ass."

I'm pretty sure I *do* want another round of his hand and my ass, despite the fact that it hurt more than I expected. He definitely didn't hold back much. "Yes," I admit.

"You have a thing for fire, Sparks?"

I rub my lips together again. "I might."

"Okay, this is what I want to know, little dragon. Why do I have a pyro working in my firehouse?"

I stop breathing and my body goes rigid beneath him. My heart pounds harder than it has since he came in here.

29

His keen blue gaze arrests me. I'd pegged him for a grumpy but hot meat-head, but the Blaze I see now has way more perception and depth than I gave him credit for. It's like he sees right into my soul.

He changes his grip to hold both my wrists in one of his large hands, then strokes his thumb over the frantic pulse in my neck. "Relax," he soothes and I find myself calming. "Nothing bad is going to happen here. It's just you and me. And you're going to come clean."

Burning leaps behind my eyes like I'm going to cry, but there's also the sense of something letting go in my chest. Something that's been caged there for so long I didn't realize it was trapped.

And that's when the alarm rings.

"Fuck." Blaze rises, lifting me to my feet in less than two seconds. "Not with those panties," he growls and literally tears them down my legs.

There's no time to argue. We have fifty-seven seconds to get the truck out of here. I jump commando into my pants and boots and yank them on. As Blaze trucks out of my room, I see him slip my panties in his pocket. Something warm swirls around my chest. I have to force myself to move because the desire to stand there and replay every single touch and word spoken between us over-whelms me.

I slide down the pole, throw on my turnout and climb in behind the wheel. Then we're out—Blaze, Rocket, Cole, Scott and I, each with our assigned positions, ready to roll.

It's not until hours later—long past our shift—when the fire in a Chinese restaurant is finally out and we're all leaving the station, that the captain calls my name.

"Yeah?" I turn, my ponytail whipping around too fast.

He strides forward, glancing at the retreating backs of the rest of the crew. "We weren't done talking, Sparks. We'll pick it back up —away from the station. Tomorrow night."

My heart thuds against my sternum. I love that he doesn't ask—
he tells. It's so in line with his personality and what we just did that
it sends spirals of heat plowing through my body.

"Yeah, okay. I live alone."

Stupid. I don't know why I said that. He didn't say he wanted to
have sex. Or maybe that's exactly what he meant. I don't know!
Finish our conversation could mean a lot of things.

His sensual lips twitch. "Great. I'll text you for the address."

I try my best for nonchalant, even though I feel like I might've
just won the lottery. I've literally never been this excited about a
guy. "I'll be waiting."

"Good." He turns and I watch his strong back retreat.

Shazam.

But I shouldn't get excited. Blaze is a tight-ass who plays by the
rules. He probably wants to tell me we can never, ever get frisky
again.

I'll have to convince him otherwise.

CHAPTER 4

laze

Lia's on the fourth floor—no elevator, but the building seems secure—I have to get buzzed in. Of course, her cop brothers would probably insist on safety. She doesn't need me to do the security check.

Not that it will stop me.

I climb the stairs and knock on her door.

And then I nearly die.

Because Lia answers in a pair of painted on jeans and skin-tight crop top—not trashy, though. Fancy, with ruffles around the little cap sleeves and the short hem. It makes her boobs look twice as juicy as they do in her FDNY shirt. A pair of sexy high heeled sandals completes the look and forces me to wipe the drool off my chin.

I have plans for her—a dinner date. A serious talk.

Maybe some more heavy petting—I haven't made my mind up about that, yet. I shouldn't engage this way. I really can't let this go any further. This conversation should be about making sure we never touch each other again.

But I already know that's not gonna happen.

And my plans all go out the fourth story window when I see her. I snatch her up to me, claim her mouth like it's always been mine. Like she was trying to keep it from me and I need to prove to her exactly who has ownership. And exactly how I intend to exercise my rights.

Her lips are impossibly soft. Supple. Tantalizing. I lick them open and thrust my tongue in her mouth, moving from zero to ninety in these five seconds. She bites my lower lip, gives it back to me. My hand cups her face, the other her squeezable ass. The same ass I got to spank to a pretty pink last night.

I still can't believe it.

Somehow, I remember my plan. And then I try to forget it, because, damn, she tastes so good.

"I have condoms." She's breathless, pulling me inside the still-open door.

Her suggestion is enough to jerk me out of my lust-induced reverie. "Whoa, whoa, whoa. Wait." I pull away and step back onto her doorstep. "That's not why I came here."

"It's not?" A mask falls over her face and I instantly curse my lack of charm. I never had any game with females. I'm too direct. Too serious. Way too controlling, as my ex-girlfriend Samantha was quick to point out. And I have a tendency to jump into things too fast—a habit Samantha also made me regret.

"Well, maybe it is," I amend, "but I wanted to take you out. Can I take you out, Sparks?"

Her lips spread into a wide smile. "Sure. Yeah."

"Let's go, then. You ready?"

"Yep. She picks up her purse from a hook on the wall. "Where are we going?"

I offer my hand and she takes it—the tough girl from the station replaced by pure sweetness. Her hand feels small, soft. I love having it captured in mine—that she trusts me enough for the simple, but intimate connection. "It's a surprise," I say, more than a little nervous about my choice, even though it's a perfectly nice restaurant. It's just been a while since I've had a date.

Since Samantha moved out and took the kid I helped raise from my life without a backward glance.

Lia comes easily, though. No more questions, no arguments. Just like in her room at the station, she accepts my direction, my dominance. She may be made of sass and spitfire courage, but submission turns her on. I'm sure of it.

The question is—what am I going to do about it?

Cards on the table—I have several lurid ideas. I just know I shouldn't suggest them.

Dating Lia is totally off-limits. Not only does she work at the station, but I'm her boss. And yet, the idea of shutting whatever's between us down has me ready to quit my job just to fuck her.

Too fast, dipshit. Way too fast.

I hail a cab downstairs and give the address to an upscale restaurant near my place. She smiles as we're seated, and I fucking love seeing her face open, her shoulders relaxed. The guys at the station have her on constant edge, ready to defend or prove herself. I hope she doesn't feel that way with me. I wince a little remembering how gruff I've been with her. Yeah, I haven't done anything to help her feel welcome, have I? It's just now that she's let me spank her beautiful ass that I consider her feelings.

"Hey, I'm sorry I've been a dick at work," I say. "I'm not trying to ride your ass, I've just been worried—"

"Worried?" she cuts in, the tension returning. I curse myself for screwing this up again.

I hold my palms out. "Not that you can't do the job. I know you can. I guess you just inspire something protective in me, that's all. I'm a fucking Neanderthal—what can I say? I worry more about keeping you safe than I do the other assholes."

Her green eyes narrow and study me. "That's sexist."

"I know—I'm sorry. I'm not saying it's right. Just trying to explain where I was coming from. I'll work on it. Promise."

The waitress shows up and asks what we'd like to drink.

"Do you drink wine?" I ask Lia.

"Yeah, sure."

"White or red?"

"White."

I order a bottle of white. I'm usually a beer guy, but I'm trying to do this right. After the waitress has served it, Lia leans forward. "So, is this a date?"

"No," I say, too abruptly. Her expression turns blank again and I hurry to say, "I mean, *this*"—I point between her and me—"isn't happening at all. As far as anyone else knows." I cock a brow. "Right?"

Her reluctant smile appears. "Absolutely. Nothing happening." She locks her lips and mimes throwing away the key. She's cute as hell when she's not trying to prove something.

"Listen, I know I shouldn't be here. I broke a million rules yesterday with you, and I could definitely lose my job over this."

"But here you are."

"Yeah. I sure as hell couldn't let that ride without..." I hesitate, trying to make sure the words come out right. I'm not good with this shit. "—without connecting with you again. In private."

She takes a sip of wine and grimaces.

I laugh. "Is it bad?"

She smiles. "Just not used to it."

"It's not really my thing, either. Next time I'll take you out for wings and a beer."

She grins and lifts her glass to clink mine. "Cheers to that."

We order our food and she steals glances at me over the top of her wine glass. "Do you always feel like you have to take a girl out after you spank her ass?"

I choke on my water and cough, hiding my mouth with my napkin.

I'm saved from answering by the waitress bringing our food— her chicken, my steak. I watch her eat, enjoying her healthy appetite. She may be small, but her metabolism must be off the charts, because she cleans her plate in about five minutes flat.

When we finish, I insist on ordering dessert, because of the way she perked up when the waitress mentioned it.

Finally, I broach the subject I've been toying with since yesterday. "So, Lia. About the pyromania."

Her fork, loaded with flourless chocolate torte, freezes on the way to her mouth.

"I could propose a theory that you chose to be a firefighter because you're enamored with flames, but I think it's something else. Something deeper."

She sets the fork down, the morsel of dessert uneaten.

"I used to work over on Staten Island. Ladder number 153."

Lia

OH GOD.

I'm sure all the blood drains from my face. My dinner I so enjoyed turns into a rock in my belly.

Blaze goes on, "I remember a cop's house burned down. There was a teenage girl."

Damn the tears that pop into my eyes. I blink them back.

Blaze signals for the check and picks up my hand. "That's a lot to carry, little girl," he murmurs softly.

I can't breathe—can't look into his steady blue gaze. I drop my eyes to the table. He knows about our fire. Could he have guessed it was all my fault?

"Lotta guilt."

My head jerks back up. Jesus. He put it together.

Everything.

The secret I've kept all these years. The reason I have to make it work as a firefigher, have to redeem myself, make sure I atone for my sins.

He doesn't seem accusatory, though. There's sympathy in his eyes, but also a firmness, like he's not about to let me get away with lying, or hiding from my past.

My lips tremble. "What is this?"

He shrugs his sculpted shoulders. "As your captain, I need to know your motivations and your weaknesses. We work as a team. Our lives are literally in each other's hands."

The crowded restaurant swoops around me. I pull a steadying breath through my nostrils and manage to nod. "Wow. I didn't expect this."

"I don't want you acting the hero because you have to make up for some past crime you can't get over, Lia. You won't make the right decisions. You'll endanger yourself and the rest of us."

I draw back, stung. Is he saying he can't keep me on the job after all? What kind of horrible non-date is this?

"I'd like to see you work through this shit fast."

"And how do you propose I do that?"

"Submit for punishment and wipe the slate clean."

I sit there blinking for a moment, replaying his words to make sense of them.

"Punishment?" I finally croak. What is he suggesting? I turn myself into the cops? To my dad? What are they going to do—investigate a crime I committed when I was thirteen?

That's when I see the corners of his lips turn up. The wicked gleam in his eyes.

And suddenly, my panties are soaked. My nipples harden like diamonds.

"Holy shit. You mean submit to you?" My pussy literally clenches, like his fingers are inside me again.

He doesn't move, just watches me with that all-seeing blue gaze. But then I see he's not breathing and I realize he's sweating this moment as much as I am.

Sure he is. If I react badly—if I tell anyone about this conversation—anyone at all—he'll lose his job and reputation in a flash. And just like that, the power shifts back to me.

I pick up my discarded fork and take a seductive bite of dessert. "And what would this punishment entail, Captain?"

He shifts in his seat like his dick got hard and he has to make room for it in his pants.

Good.

"Three spankings. Serious ones—the kind that leave your ass sore the next day."

OMG, OMG, OMG. I want to put my fingers between my legs *right now* to alleviate the throb there.

"Will there..." I clear my throat. "Will they have a happy ending?"

His lips curve up. "I promise if you take it like a good girl, there will be plenty of rewards."

Pussy clench.

"Wow." Heat feathers across my face and I become very interested in forking up my next bite of torte.

"Lia, I think you're excited about my proposal, but if you feel at all obligated—like I'm your boss and you have to do this to keep the job—tell me to fuck off right now. Because if you're not one hundred percent on board, I will never, ever mention any of this again. In fact, you can think of this conversation as your job security, because you pretty much have me by the balls now."

I relax a bit. I wasn't feeling obligated, but I love that he's making himself as vulnerable to me as I feel with him right now.

"Seriously—this could be the worst sexual harassment case the FDNY ever saw. Which is pretty ripe considering I've been worried about keeping the other guys from making you uncomfortable."

I take my last bite of dessert and set the fork down. "I'm in. I'm totally in." I meet his gaze squarely.

The connection between us is electric. His lips quirk up.

"And I'm kinda terrified."

"I'm pretty sure that's part of the thrill." He throws some money on the table and stands. His arm loops around my waist when I stand. "I promise I'll take care of you, Sparks. Do you believe that?"

I look up into his rugged face. Do I? Can I trust this guy with my body? My pride?

I think of how he managed me yesterday—not just the sex part, but the way he pinned me down to get the truth out of me. If only someone in my family had done that for me after the fire. Just pinned me down and asked what I knew. If I'd started it.

Would my life have been easier?

Hell, yes.

"Yeah, I believe it." I reach around his waist and pat his rock hard ass. "Besides, I have you by the balls, right?"

His deep laugh is rich and it warms me from the inside. "Exactly, Sparks. As it should be."

After a cab ride back to my place, he walks me to the door. When he doesn't follow me in, I turn and lean in the door frame.

"Did you want to come in?"

"No. Tonight I'm going to kiss you at the door and send you to bed. We're working tomorrow and I need you fresh. Next Tuesday when we're on our three day break, I want you at my place at 7 p.m. sharp, ready to submit. If you don't show, I'll assume you changed your mind and I'll never say another word about it. Understand?"

I nod.

"I need a *yes, sir.*"

Pussy clench.

I lean into his space so my breasts brush his shirt. "Yes... *Daddy.*"

His eyes darken. He snatches me up against him and claims my mouth with the same fervor he showed at the beginning of the evening. One hand palms my ass. I lift a leg and wrap it around his waist. Well, more like his thighs, because I can't reach his waist.

I know he wants me—the evidence of his arousal pushes against my stomach—but he eases me back with a groan.

"Fuck, you taste so sweet. I can't wait to find out if the rest of you tastes this good." He moves back in, cupping my mons, rubbing the knuckle of his thumb over my clit.

I cry out, already close to orgasm, just from our conversation and the kissing.

He steps back again, though, smacking my pussy through my jeans. "Here's a rule you'd better heed—no pleasure until after punishment. This pussy belongs to me. Don't touch her unless I give you permission." He reaches out and tweaks one of my nipples through my blouse. "I know you're excited. You can think about how you'll be punished, but no touching. You're just going to have to let that energy build so you're primed and ready for it when the time comes."

I let out a growl of frustration and Blaze rubs my ear between his fingers, then tugs it gently.

41

"What do you say?"

"Yes, Daddy." He liked it when I called him that last time. I'm not going to stop.

"Good girl. I promise I'll make it worth it, Sparks." He winks at me and steps back to shut the door.

Oh lordy. How will I survive until Tuesday? I'm already ready to explode!

CHAPTER 5

laze

By Monday, I'm supercharged. I've worked two more shifts with my little pyro, and I can't wait to get my hands on her again.

I may have told Lia not to touch herself, but I didn't hold myself to the same standard. And believe me, it was for everyone's highest good. The team does not need a blue-balled captain running the show. I figure I'm doing the city a favor by jerking off twice a day to relieve the pressure.

Every time I even think about what's going to happen Tuesday I get a boner the size of Lady Liberty. I'm also putting most of my mental energy into planning the date. Yeah, I'm calling it a date.

It's the best kind of fantasy date I can imagine.

I guess that makes me the kinky motherfucker my ex-fiancée Samantha always accused me of being.

I have some weird dominance kink. Sure, I'm an alpha male in all aspects of my life. And I'm definitely protective—over-protective is what Samantha called me. But I'm also... kinked. Not sadistic. Not really. But spanking a girl gets me harder than a rock.

And I fucking love the idea of spanking her for real. Not just a couple slaps as foreplay, but a full-on punishment. The kind that leaves her begging for mercy and wide-eyed with submission.

Don't try to get me to explain why.

There is no why.

It's just the way I'm wired.

And before I saw the way Lia lit up over the idea of punishment, I thought it made me a sick bastard. That's why she's almost too good to be true. That's why I can't leave the girl alone, despite the risk to my career.

Because it's like the moment I recognized the twin flame in her, the ember of mine flared to life. I'd been smothering it. Starving it for oxygen.

But suddenly it seemed acceptable. Not just acceptable—actually welcomed. A thing to be enjoyed. A thing that could give Lia pleasure.

And that gave me the headiest power rush I've ever had.

Possibly even more than saving lives or putting out fires.

I'm tempted to get her alone today, whisper all the dirty things I want to do to her, but I can't risk it. It's bad enough it's my night to cook and she's hanging around like she wants to help.

I chose ribs. It's my favorite and can't be ruined easily by the inevitable call because it's a slow bake in the oven. The worst for ruined dinner is steak. Or pasta. If a call comes in while you're in the middle of cooking those, you can just kiss your meal goodbye.

I unwrap the first package of meat, rinse it and slap it down on a huge sheet of tinfoil.

"Captain's going all out tonight," Rocket observes, stripping the husk off the two dozen ears of corn we bought. The guys like to give me shit because ribs are expensive and we all split the cost of food, but I know they love it.

Lia hovers a few feet away. I register her presence viscerally, as I'm sure every male in the station does. It's like I come alive around her, the alpha male in me eager to show off, stake my claim, throw down the competition. I haven't felt this way in a long time. After Samantha, and the heartbreak of losing my little ready-made family unit, complete with a kid, I guess I wrote off women. Which is pretty lame considering I'm only thirty-six.

"So you gonna graduate me from dish duty tonight or what?" she demands. Her voice is sultry, like honeyed iced tea on a hot day.

I turn and frown, only because I sense an actual smile wanting to appear. Lord knows it would break my face.

"No rookies in the kitchen," Rocket says flatly.

Our official rule is that newbies aren't allowed to cook. They're given dish duty. Cooking for the team is something they work up to as the trust builds. It strikes me as an idiotic rule at the moment.

"If you want to help me, you can," I find myself saying.

"Wouldn't be showing a gender bias, would you, Captain?" This from the damn peanut gallery, otherwise known as James.

I toss a scowl his way.

Lia ignores us both and steps up to my side, unwrapping another package of ribs. "I love cooking," she breezes, pretending there's no tension over her presence here. "My mom is Puerto Rican. Cooking is an expression of love for her." She's already slapping down ribs like she's a butcher's wife. She tips her head up to look at me. "You have a special recipe, Captain?"

I stare down at her big green eyes, fascinated with the gold flecks, the long, naturally dark lashes. For a moment, I can't think of anything but how much I'd like her cooking special meals just for me, serving them up with her as dessert. I pull another scowl to cover. "Just barbecue sauce."

"Mmm." She makes a non-committal sound and starts opening cabinets. Pretty soon she's rubbing the meat with some kind of olive oil and spice concoction before she folds the foil up into neat little packages.

"Little hint, Sparks," Rocket says to Lia. "You're not supposed to make the captain look bad. Haven't you wondered why we call him Blaze?"

"Temper?" She steals a look at me.

"Yep."

Her nipples bead up under her t-shirt. I almost growl out loud, thinking that the other guys might notice.

"I'm not afraid of him," she says lightly, inciting a chorus of "oohs" from the guys.

"Oh you should be, little gi—"

Damn. I *cannot* call her *little girl* around here.

I clear my throat. "I mean, uh, Sparks."

James snorts. "You're so worried about *us* getting the department slapped with a harassment suit."

Lia pops the ribs in the oven and starts washing the lettuce for the salad.

"Are you telling me strip poker was a good idea?"

He shrugs. He's the one who bitched the loudest when I told him they hired a female for the vacant position. It's his cousin J.J. who Lia replaced after J.J. fell off the ladder and broke his back. He survived. He may even walk again. But it will be a long slow recovery and he won't ever join us or any other crew again. We're all sorry as hell he was hurt on the job. "I don't think any of this is a good idea."

Lia turns slowly. "Any of what, exactly?" Her chin lifts, green eyes pin him.

James scowls and stands up like he's disgusted with her and the whole conversation. "You have no idea what this job is about, do you?" he snarls.

The certainty slips from her expression for a moment, and I'm relieved she realizes there's more to this than sexism. She glances at me and I give my head a small shake.

Her gaze slips back to James. "I'm hoping to learn," she says simply.

James snorts and leaves the room.

I'm dying to wrap Lia up in my arms, but, of course, I can't. Rocket's up behind her, dropping a hand on her shoulder. I should be grateful the rest of the crew has some sympathy, but the sight of him touching her makes my fingers curl into fists.

And of course, that's when the alarm sounds, ending any chance for explanations or discussion.

~

Lia

I CALL my cousin Talia on the way to Blaze's.

"Hey, girl. How's the new job?"

I close my eyes, grateful for her enthusiasm. As the only girl in a male-dominated family, I latched onto my older cousin like we were sisters. She spent a couple summers with us when she was a teen and I stayed with her for a few months after I graduated high school—when I was trying to figure out what to do with my life. She pretty much got me on the track that led me here. I sometimes joke that she's my life coach.

"Hey. It's good. Hard, but good."

"Yeah? Have you made any friends yet? Are your co-workers hot? Or is it wrong to perv on firemen when you're one of them?"

I laugh. "Actually..." I drag the last syllable out.

"Ooh. This sounds interesting. Did you make a special friend?"

"Okay, wow. You read into this situation way too fast. Um, yeah. I have a date tonight with the captain."

"A date? Is that allowed?"

I get off the subway and walk up the street with the phone glued to my ear. "No! It's totally not allowed. But we had this kind of incredible magnetic attraction. We both agreed not to tell anyone. Do you think I'm crazy?"

"I think you should be careful," she hedges. "You worked really hard to get this job. But if anything happens to affect your job, we'll find you a good lawyer and sue the FDNY for sexual harassment."

"Yeah, and he pretty much admitted he was opening himself up for that, so I think I'm safe. We both know what we're messing with."

"You sound good."

I smile, even though she can't see it. "I do? Thanks. I'm excited. And nervous."

"So what are you doing for the date?"

"Um." I don't want to tell her this part. I mean how do you say, *it's not really a date, it's kinky spank play that I can't even begin to understand my attraction to?* "I don't know yet—he's in charge." *Not a lie.* "I'm almost there, just wanted to say hey in person. Thanks for listening."

"My pleasure. Have fun on the date. Text me to let me know you got home okay later."

"I will—thanks!" I end the call just as I reach Blaze's building. He texted me his address along with the instructions to wear panties like the ones I had on for my last spanking. The ones he kept.

Has he been thinking about that scene as much as I have?

I ring the bell. He buzzes me in and I climb the stairs to his apartment and stand in front of his door.

I'm wearing a pair of leggings and a t-shirt. I went for easy removal—hope I made the right choice! My knees are knocking even more than they did my first day on the job. The day I showed up to a very grouchy captain and a crew who didn't want me.

This is a totally different kind of nervous, though. It's the exciting kind, with the butterflies dancing around and heat thrumming between my legs. I knock.

He answers, looking sexy as hell in a worn pair of jeans and a tight, fitted t-shirt that shows off every line of his sculpted torso.

I lick my lips and his gaze tracks the movement. "Hey."

He pulls me inside and shuts the door. "Hey, yourself. I'm glad you came."

His place is nice—small, but very clean and neat, with decent furniture. A little on the spartan side.

"Were you worried I wouldn't?"

He reaches for a lock of my hair, which I wore down tonight, and twists it around his finger. "I might've sweated it a bit. You ready for your punishment?"

I nod. My mind's been going crazy over the past four days since our date, trying to figure out what this all means. What's Blaze's deal? Is he only in this for the kink? He offered me the option of coming or having him never mention it again. Us dating the normal way wasn't on the table.

Or am I overanalyzing this?

Probably.

He lifts his chin toward an open door. "The bedroom's in there. I want you to go in, shut the door, and take off all your clothes but your panties. If you need to use the restroom, do that first. Then kneel in the corner and wait for me."

The flutters in my belly surge, my whole pelvic floor lifts and squeezes. This is really happening.

He's serious.

Part of me wants to run for the door as fast as I can.

49

But I'm no chicken.

And besides, I want this.

It's way more than a curiosity. Way beyond seeing what makes the captain tick. This is for me. When he mentioned punishment, something I never knew was inside me woke up. It was like he was speaking a secret language to me.

And yes, absolution for my sins sounds wonderful.

So does having it delivered by the sexy captain.

"Yes, sir." I walk on wobbly knees to the bedroom and shut the door. This room is like the rest of the place. Clean. Comfortable. Simple.

I feel like I'm at the doctor's office, where you strip as fast as you can because the thought of not being in the appropriate garb when the doctor comes back is embarrassing.

I want to get this right.

Do whatever Blaze asks of me.

And yeah, the kneeling gave me pause. But only for a second. And then it turned me way the hell on.

I take off my clothes and fold them up. In the corner, I see he's put a small pillow on the floor.

It's so freaking thoughtful, my chest tightens. Heart pounding, I drop to my knees on it, facing the juncture of the two walls.

Blaze comes in and shuts the door. I listen for his footsteps, but they don't come to me, they head toward the bed.

"Come here, little girl."

I stand up, heat burning my cheeks. It's one thing to play sexy cock tease and goad him into spanking me at the station. It's quite another to be called on the carpet this way. The fact that I'm almost completely naked and he's fully dressed makes it all the more squirmy, which I'm sure is his intent.

Still, he's warm. Almost inviting. He spreads his knees wide and reaches for me, pulling me to stand between them. He cups my ass in his hands, kneading possessively.

"Do you know what a safe word is?"

I nod.

"I need a *yes, sir.*"

"Yes, Daddy."

His lips twitch. "What's yours, baby?"

I nibble my lip. "Um... fire truck."

Another quirk of his sexy mouth. "Fire truck. Got it." He continues to squeeze my cheeks roughly, inciting a flare of heat so powerful it's a wonder I remain on my feet. When he pulls me closer and applies his lips to one of my nipples, I let out a wanton moan.

He sucks and flicks it with his tongue, then scraps lightly with his teeth. "I know you might be reluctant to call it, so I'm going to be careful with you, Sparks. I'll be paying attention. Okay?" He applies his lips to my neglected nipple, which sends a zing straight between my legs.

I drop my head back and pant, and my brain doesn't process that he asked me a question. Or maybe I thought it was rhetorical.

He slaps my ass lightly and raises his brows.

"Oh, um, yes, sir!"

He releases his delicious grip on my ass and gathers my wrists behind my back. It thrusts my breasts forward and he feasts on my nipple once more.

I shift, twitching my inner thighs against one another, seeking relief.

"Were you a good girl this week, Lia?" He scrapes his teeth lightly over my beaded nipple again.

"Um..." I'm panting, hardly coherent.

"Did you touch your pussy?"

"Oh! No. I was good, I promise."

He makes an approving hum and pulls me down over one leg so my torso rests on the bed, my ass is draped up over his knee, raised and angled perfectly for his hand.

Yum.

Or so I think, but then the first swat falls.

Harder than I expect.

It's like it was in the station—a little too much. A little hurtier than I want, but not enough to mind. I wriggle over his knee, trying to dodge the firm slaps. He holds my wrists caged at my lower back and slaps my ass over and over again.

"Why am I punishing you, little girl?" His deep voice reverberates through my body.

I whimper, not from the pain, but from the question. I really don't want to talk about this. It will definitely take all the fun out of this experience.

"Were you playing with matches?"

Okay, that's still fun. It has way more of a naughty girl vibe to it than *Did you burn down your parents' house with your family still in it? Did you leave permanent scars on your mother's arm? Did you destroy all the family photos, heirlooms and property just because you have a fascination with fire?*

"Yes, sir," I gasp, suddenly wanting it harder. Wishing he'd spank this fire, this wicked obsession right out of me, forevermore.

He spanks me with steady, firm smacks and each one seems to reach that deep hidden place inside me, the one where I stuffed the darkness, tried to pretend it didn't exist. It penetrates to the cache of guilt, the horror, the burden I carry every day.

I moan but not from pain. More from satisfaction. Because it feels so right to receive this discipline, the hard, stinging smacks, the relentless focus on my redemption.

"No more, Lia." His voice is firm, almost a touch angry. "Not in my fire station. Not at home. No. More. Matches."

I stop breathing, don't even move except for the involuntary jerk of my hips under his smacks.

Is he really asking me to give up my matches?

I can't!

"Did you hear me?"

I don't answer, because I can't. I'm choked up, a little frightened of the magnitude of what he's asking.

He pulls me back up to stand, cupping my hot ass in his hands. His touch is gentle this time, not the hot, rough kneading of before, but gentle squeezes. "Look at me."

I can't meet his eyes.

"Lia."

I swallow and drag my gaze from his shirt to his face.

"You can do this."

Oh God, he *understands*. The fact that he knows how big his demand is, that he doesn't just think I'm being defiant, makes this easier.

"You want to light a match, you come see me. I'll give you what you need."

My stomach flutters, wondering if *this* is what he thinks I need. More punishment. More pain.

I think he may be right.

I give a wobbly nod. "Okay." It comes out as no more than a whisper.

"That's my girl." Blaze pulls me into him, as if for an embrace, but he affixes his lips to my right nipple again. I clutch the back of his head and wiggle my hips.

He pulls his lips off with a pop and pushes my hips back a few inches. Then he hooks his thumbs in the waistband of my panties.

My breath hitches as he pulls them slowly down to my thighs. I got a Brazilian two days ago in preparation for this date at the advice of my bestie from high school. She's a hairstylist and swears by waxing for a hot date.

Judging by the expression on Blaze's face, I'd say she was right.

"Oh, baby," he croaks, lightly running the pad of his thumb over the smooth seam of my pussy. "Did you do this for me?"

53

"I did," I murmur, slowly swaying my hips, trying to get my panties to drop the rest of the way.

Blaze groans. "Not yet, baby. Your punishment isn't over. I need to spank you with your panties down now."

Ho boy! I'm not sure why that's exciting to me, but it totally is. I let him arrange me back over his left knee, moisture seeping between my thighs.

He starts spanking again and it's even better than before. Yes, it's stingier because my panties are down, but I've had a chance to get used to the sensation now, and I welcome each smack as if he were delivering pleasure, rather than pain.

I now totally understand how people can get off on pain. Especially—or maybe only—when it's delivered by someone who's ultimately interested in pleasure. Both his and mine.

I surrender more to the sensation, to Blaze.

He spanks harder, which makes me realize he was holding back before, warming me up slowly.

God bless him.

And holy shit! The man can smack hard.

I'm juicy wet with arousal, squirming for release, but it seems like he'll never stop. My ass is on fire and yet each smack feels like it's not enough. I want more. Harder.

"Blaze," I moan.

He stops spanking, rubbing a slow circle over my twitching ass. "Are you okay, baby?"

"Yes," I breathe. "I need—"

"Tell me what you need."

"More." I almost curse the word as it tumbles from my lips. "You," I say quickly, to cover it up.

"You'll get both." He pulls me up to stand and tugs my panties the rest of the way off. "Kneel in the corner again."

I do it. I don't even hesitate. I guess that means I really trust this guy. Or else I'm too horny to argue. I hear him moving around the room, hear the jingle of metal.

"Come here, baby."

When I turn around, I see he's built a mound of pillows in the middle of the bed. Leather cuffs with buckles and chains are attached to the corners of the bed.

My clit throbs and my knees almost buckle.

"This is going to be the hardest part of your punishment, baby. But when it's over, I promise I'll reward you. All night long, if you want."

My cheeks heat even as a smile stretches my lips.

He pats the pillows. I have no doubt what he intends, and I comply without complaint, draping my body over them so my ass is lifted high in the air. He binds each wrist and ankle to the bed restraints and I'm now naked, spread eagle and presented for his punishment.

What will it be?

He grips both my asscheeks and spreads them wide.

I'm surprised and try to squeeze them closed and he smacks my ass. "Let me look at this ass and pussy. You made yourself all smooth for me." He makes that hum of approval and I'm instantly wagging my ass like I have a tail or am offering myself up to him.

He smacks lightly between my legs. "How's this little pussy doing? Is she wet for me?" He smacks again. "She is, isn't she?"

Oh god.

"I might need to make her suffer a bit before your reward."

"No," I moan, not even sure what he's talking about.

He smacks my ass again. "You don't tell me no." I hear the buzz of electronics and identify the sound just before the vibrator probes my lips.

I jerk and moan. It's too much. Especially if I'm not going to get relief yet. I'm already horned up beyond belief. This will kill me. Literally.

"Please," I moan.

"Use my name when you beg me, baby."

"Please, Blaze?"

"Sorry, Sparks. Not yet." He teases my opening with the buzzing device, then pushes it in.

I cry out, so close to orgasm, but then he doesn't move it.

I mean, he just *leaves it there.* Torturing me.

Cruel, cruel man.

Blaze

LIA'S BLOWING my fucking mind. I'm not surprised—she always does. I'm working hard to make sure this goes well. I would feel awful if I made her uncomfortable or did something that left her feeling worse about the fire she set rather than better.

But so far, everything's been perfect—like we're playing the same game. And even though I'm the one in charge here, she's rocking my world.

Christ, the sight of her now!

She looks incredible, twisting against her cuffs, her breath moving the muscles of her slender, muscular back. I stained her ass pink but it's not mottled or showing any signs of marking. Not that I have enough experience to know. No girl has let me go this far.

Heh. That makes it sound like I'm sixteen making it to third base. Well, I'm about as ready to blow as a teenager, that's for sure.

She humps the bed, like she's trying to get more friction from the vibrator. I'm so tempted to let her come.

But not yet.

I unbuckle my belt and pull it through the loops.

She turns her head to watch me, eyes rounded.

I give her a moment, in case she wants to safe word.

She undulates her hips.

Okay, she's still turned on. Not overly scared.

Good.

I slowly wrap the buckle end of the belt around my hand. The idea of whipping her both excites and terrifies me.

I want to hear the slap of leather against her skin. Hear her cry out in pain, or beg me for mercy. But I need this to be what she craves, too. If I take this too far, I'll never forgive myself.

"I'm going to whip you now, little girl. You have my permission to come."

Excitement flares in her eyes.

"Ready?"

"Yes, sir." Her voice warbles—whether from fear or excitement, I'm not sure. Probably a mixture of both.

I bring the belt down across her ass, tempering the stroke.

Her hips jerk and she squeezes her cheeks together. She moans. I whip her again. She humps the pillows. She's enjoying it.

"I'm going to whip your ass raw, little girl. And when I'm done, you'll promise me you've learned your lesson."

"Yes," she gasps, squeezing her ass again when I slap the leather across her bare cheeks. "Oh, Blaze."

I whip her again.

"Ouch. Yes. It hurts," she moans, but her tone sounds wanton. Like *it hurts* is a good thing. I don't stop.

"Blaze," she moans. "Blaze... please. Blaze."

Fuck.

The way she's moaning my name makes my cock throb to the point of pain.

"Do you need my cock inside you when you come, baby?" My voice sounds rough—I almost don't recognize it. I sure as hell didn't expect such crude words to come out of my mouth.

"Yes," she answers immediately. "Yes, yes, yes, yes."

And it's all over.

I throw the belt on the floor and yank out my cock, sheathing it with a lubricated condom. I pull the vibrator out, but don't turn it off, instead I wedge it beneath her, so it hits her clit.

"You ready for me?" I growl. "It's going to be rough."

"Ready. I'm ready, I'm ready," she chants.

I freaking love this girl.

I do my best to hold back as I push in. I know I'm big, and—fuck—she's tiny, but she's slick and welcoming. I don't think I'm going to fit at first—she's tight. So tight! But I grit my teeth to keep from ramming home and work it in slowly.

"Please, please, please, Blaze." She pushes her hot, red ass back at me like she wants it deep.

My eyes flip back in my head and I start mindlessly pumping.

She feels. So. Good.

Incredible.

Tight and wet and *perfect*.

I love this girl. I'm not kidding.

"Lia," I murmur. "Tell me if I hurt you."

She's gripping the straps that bind her to the bed, knuckles white. The muscles in her back are corded up with strain. "It's good," she pants. "It's so good."

Thank fuck.

Even though she's not going anywhere—I made damn sure of that when I cuffed her—I hold her down by the nape. I jack-hammer into her with hard, brutal thrusts. I can't help myself. Nothing's felt so good in my entire life.

"Lia," I snarl, my balls tightening, thighs quaking.

"Please, Blaze, please," she pleads.

Her begging pushes me over the edge. I slam in deep. "Come, Lia," I bark roughly. I'm already screaming my climax, cum filling the condom as I shudder over her. I grind down, forcing her clit more firmly against the vibrator and she breaks.

"Blaze—oh *God!*" Her pussy squeezes my dick, extending my climax, wringing even more out of me.

Her tiny body bucks, breath chokes and gasps. It's a sound I want to hear every fucking night for the rest of my life. From this dream girl who takes my kink and wears it like she owns it.

I pull out and dispose of the condom, then quickly unbuckle her cuffs. She's gone limp and I roll her over, pulling out the pillows and covering her body with my own. I kiss her like I own her. I'm grateful—soaring on that high that comes with the best orgasm of my life, and I want her to feel it, too.

She responds, wrapping her legs around my waist, pulling me down with her slender arms around my neck. Before I know it, I'm inside her again, only bareback this time.

It feels incredible.

I can't.

I shouldn't.

And I don't want to stop.

"I'm sorry," I groan, still rocking in and out of her, claiming her mouth like my life depends on it. "I didn't know I'd get hard again so fast."

It's a lame excuse, but maybe she'll take it as a compliment.

"I'm clean, I swear. I'll get you the paperwork."

She shoves a bit at my chest and I snap back to reality and pull out. "I'm sorry," I say again, then make it up to her by kissing down her neck, between her breasts, along the flat plane of her belly.

I hook my hands under her knees and spread her open.

Her pussy is fucking beautiful. I wouldn't have said I liked the all-bare thing, but on her it's a miracle. I lick into her.

She shudders, hands flying to my head, hips rolling up to meet my face.

I treat her to the best head I know how to give, tracing inside her outer lips, teasing her clit, penetrating her with my tongue. I suck on her clit and slip my thumb in, my middle finger sliding back to her anus.

She jerks and comes the moment I touch it, which causes my rock hard dick to become steel. When the flutters of her muscles relax and she eases her grip on my hair, I pull away.

"Next time I discipline you, I'm going to take your ass," I murmur, massaging a slow circle over her anus.

The ring of muscles squeezes under my finger and she whimpers.

I kiss up her belly again. "You okay?"

She pushes up on her forearms. "More than okay."

I didn't realize I was still nervous until the relief pours through me. She loved it as much as I thought she did.

"Good." I climb up beside her and lie on my side, wrapping an arm around her waist.

She rolls away from me but pushes her ass into my lap, snuggling against me.

My cock throbs, dying to be inside her again, but I can tell by her slowing breaths she's going down for the count.

Within a few minutes she's asleep.

You'd think I'd sleep, too, but I'm awake for hours, trying to talk my dick down because I'm already dying for another round with her.

And all this time, I'm ignoring the voice in my head screaming, *What the hell are you doing, man?* Because I know I am way the hell out of the safe zone with this girl, and I have been from the start.

I want this way too badly.

And I've been down this road before.

Even if we didn't have the problem with working at the same station and me being her boss, I'm not the kinda guy who gets to keep the girl.

I've tried and failed.

And yet the idea of failing with Lia makes me want to burn a building down, myself.

Maybe she's rubbing off on me.

Maybe I've lost my mind.

Or maybe this is exactly what I've always needed.

CHAPTER 6

_ia_

WHEN I WAKE UP, I'm all snuggled against a huge, hairy man chest. One giant tattooed arm loops around me, his hand lightly holding my ass. My leg drapes over Blaze's thick muscled thigh and—crap —I might have been grinding against him.

Apparently he turns me on, even in his sleep.

I inhale, breathing in his masculine scent. It's like leather and Coke and something deliciously Blaze.

It's hard to stop grinding. I really want this guy again.

The memory of how quickly he wanted me again last night flashes through my mind. The way he rolled me over and started kissing me, like he couldn't stop. Like keeping his hands off me was an impossibility, even though we'd both just come.

I have to say, it was damn flattering.

I don't have a ton of experience with men. I had a boyfriend my last year of high school, first year of junior college. Then a few hookups after that relationship cooled off and died. And that's about it.

Nothing on Earth prepared me for sex with Blaze.

Do you even call it sex?

Or is there some other name when it involves spanking and being tied up and taken hard?

I don't care what you call it—I loved it.

I want more.

The thing that's confusing me, is what this all means to Blaze.

Is it only about the fetish? Is he just into someone he can spank and play daddy to?

I almost moan aloud as I realize how badly I want Blaze to daddy me. I imagine him imposing rules and enforcing them with the kind of discipline he delivered last night.

Hot.

But is that a relationship? Or just a hookup? Does he want more than this? I mean, he can't give me more, can he?

We work together. What we're doing is already forbidden. We knew from the start these were like stolen kisses.

We're scratching an itch, no more.

And with that in mind, I start to slowly peel my body from his, holding my breath to keep from waking him. I shouldn't have spent the night.

Why didn't I get dressed and head home when it was over? I can't believe I fell asleep! He was probably annoyed I hung around.

Although he didn't seem that annoyed. His arm was around me, after all. It wasn't just me plastering my body against his.

Well, mostly it was, but yeah.

I slip on my clothes and pick up my shoes, tiptoeing to the living room to put them on. I'm hopping on one foot when a tattooed arm snakes around my waist and lifts me into the air.

"Where do you think you're sneaking off to, little dragon?"

"Oh, um, I…"

He hasn't put me down yet. His breath is hot on my neck.

"There's no sneaking off. Not unless you want another trip over my knee."

Oh lordy.

My pussy squeezes. Why is it sexy when he treats me like a naughty schoolgirl?

"Do you have somewhere to go?" He finally sets me down on my feet, but doesn't release me. "I wanted to cook you breakfast."

My heart flutters.

He wanted to cook me breakfast!

That doesn't sound like it was just a hookup, does it?

"Yeah, okay. I can stay."

"Good." He kisses my neck and releases me.

I attempt to drag my fingers through my tangled hair.

"Come here," he says, taking my hand and pulling me toward the bathroom in his bedroom. He produces a new toothbrush, still in the package. "Toothbrush." He points to the counter. "Comb." He opens the cabinet below and indicates the stack of neatly folded terry cloth. "Towels." He whips the shower curtain open and tips his head toward it. "Make yourself at home. You eat pancakes?"

I grin at him, stupidly. "Yep."

He smiles back. "Great. Take a shower—freshen up. They'll be ready when you're done."

Swoon.

Damn. I am falling for this guy.

Hard.

I am so screwed.

～

Blaze

I FUCKING love taking care of Lia. I don't know why caretaking is my thing, but it probably goes with the hero complex and never feeling like I can do enough.

Regardless, Lia calling me *daddy* does something powerful to me. Makes me want to spoil her like a princess.

And spank her silly.

I want her turning those big green eyes on me like I'm her everything, the way she did last night. I want her naked and begging for release. I want her on my lap, riding me like a cowgirl. I want to be the recipient of that wide, trusting smile. The guy who makes her troubles cease and gives her a safe place to be herself. I want to know her secrets, good and bad. I want to protect her from anyone who stands in her way, anyone who tries to hurt her.

Yeah, I'll be her daddy.

In a heartbeat.

But I better figure out how in the hell I'm going to keep us a secret at work. Because the first time she's in serious danger, I'm going to lose my shit.

I make a full diner breakfast—eggs, bacon and pancakes with a chocolate chip smiley face. What? She calls me daddy, right?

When she comes out, fresh-faced and dewy, it's all I can do to keep from shoving her over the kitchen table and claiming her again. But I'm supposed to be taking care of her, so I adjust my cock and wave her into a seat.

She smiles as she slips into a chair and I place a heaping plate in front of her. "Smiley pancakes!" she squeals.

I pull a can of whipped cream from the fridge. "Want some?"

She nods but opens her mouth.

Oh fuck. I am not going to survive breakfast. I squirt spirals of whipped cream into her mouth until she waves her hand to stop me, then I pile some on her pancake while she works to swallow.

"You know how to swallow like a good girl, don't you?"

Her lips stretch into a Cheshire cat smile. "Only for you, Big Daddy."

I groan and adjust my cock again. "Eat," I order, too curtly.

She doesn't take offense. In fact, I think she enjoys my discomfort as she makes a show of licking whipped cream from her fork.

I sit across from her and watch her eat while I shovel food in my mouth. When she finishes, she reaches for my plate, starting to rise from her chair.

"Leave it. I'm taking care of you, remember?" I push my chair back from the table. "Come here." I crook a finger at her.

She shakes her head, but still obeys. "Bossy."

It gives me pause. I *am* too bossy. I know I am—it's a real flaw. It's ended other relationships. But... she doesn't seem bothered by it.

I pull her to stand between my legs and fill my hands with her ass. "How's your ass today? Still sore?"

She sways her hips slowly, her hands falling to my shoulders as I destabilize her footing. "A little. A few marks that twinge when I sit."

I watch her face closely for clues. "Was it too much?" I switch one hand and rub between her legs.

"Nope. It was just right." She lifts one knee and brings it up to my hip, bringing her tits to my face. I nip one through the shirt and slip my fingers into the waistband of her leggings.

"This is only gonna end one way. You know that, right?"

She leans forward, her breath hot on my ear. She flicks her tongue. "How's that, Daddy?"

It's on. I push her back enough to get her leggings down her hips and off her toned legs. She's wearing panties like the ones I kept. The pair that featured in every fantasy I've had since I spanked her at the station. I pull them up between her cheeks like I did that night and run my palm over her shapely cheeks. I inspect her ass, relieved to see the marks are minimal—not bruises, just a few splotchy red places. While I stroke her ass, I work the fingers of my other hand over her clit, rubbing and tapping through the thin fabric.

I peel the panties down. "From now on, you'll be subject to surprise panty-checks at the station. And let me tell you, honey, I'd better find regulation material covering this heart-stopping ass, or you'll be in deep trouble." I palm her ass with one hand and run my fingers along her sopping slit with the other. "And not the fun kind of trouble, either. I will send you home without pay. Understand?"

She climbs on my lap and unbuttons my jeans. "Yes, Daddy."

I'm hard as a rock when she pulls my cock out, and I'm pissed when I realize I don't have a condom on me again. I make a mental note to put the fuckers in every pocket of every pair of pants I own.

I lift her off my lap. "Sit here. Spread those knees wide. Yeah, like that." I arrange her in my chair. "Don't move, baby, or there will be punishment."

"What kind of punishment?"

I arch a brow and give her a mock stern look before I head to the bedroom to find a condom. When I return, she's on her knees on the chair, ass out, ready for her punishment.

"Oh, baby. You were naughty while I was gone."

"I know." She wags her ass. "I guess you'll have to teach me to obey."

I'm so hot, I swing for her ass before I even have a plan. My palm connects with her bare flesh with a loud smack. "Sugarplum, you have no idea what you do to me."

She grips the back of the chair as she turns with a naughty smile. "Oh, I might have a clue."

I smack her ass again. "You have my number, don't you, baby?"

I deliver several more light slaps until her ass turns a pretty shade of pink, then I pull her down from the chair. As much as I love the idea of taking her on her knees, I don't want it to be on a rickety wooden chair. I'd probably smash it by the time I was through.

I sit back down and sheath my cock. "Climb over me, Sparks. Show me what you've got."

My little girl loves a challenge. She straddles my waist and reaches for my cock, lining it up with her entrance. Then she raises up and lowers herself onto me. Heat tingles at the base of my spine as I sink into her tight channel.

"That's it, honey. So good," I groan. I let her undulate her hips a few times and then I take over, because I'm that kinda guy. I spread my fingers wide over her ass and pull her over my cock, directing each glide as I thrust up into her.

Her small tits bounce in my face, shifting beneath her shirt, taunting me, but I can't stop to suck them, because I'm already swimming in pleasure. So much for taking care of my girl this morning. I'm a selfish bastard who can't wait to come.

I continue to bounce her, but bring my thumb between her legs, seeking her clit. She squeals when I find it and I reach around to find her anus in the back, applying pressure to the twin pleasure centers.

"Blaze!" She sounds alarmed, like she's afraid to let go.

"Come for me, Lia." I bite her nipple through her shirt.

She screeches and bucks, her inner thighs squeezing around my waist as her pussy grabs my dick and tightens.

"That's it, little dragon. You come when you're told," I praise her and she bucks again, still coming.

I've had enough. I can't stand another second's delay. I pick her up, legs still wrapped around my waist and shove my plate to the side to lay her back on the table. I lift her ankles to my shoulders and go to town, pounding into her juicy heat like my life depends on it. I grip her thighs and thrust, push her legs backward toward her shoulders. She bends and contorts like the true athlete she is, teeth chattering from the pounding I'm giving her.

Lights flash around my periphery and I hear myself shout but then I'm lost between the ecstasy of release and the internal hum of pleasure. When my focus returns, I see Lia staring up at me, eyes wide with wonder.

"Fuck," I curse. "Are you okay?" Christ, I probably just bruised her entire back and pelvis fucking her against a hard wooden table. "Did I hurt you?" I pull her torso up until I'm standing, holding her with her legs wrapped around my waist.

"I'm okay." She sounds dazed, far away.

I carry her to my bedroom and lay her on the bed while I dispose of the condom. When I come back, I crawl over her and pin her down, dragging my mouth across her jaw to her neck, then between her breasts. I kiss and nuzzle until her breath returns to normal and her fingers tangle idly in my hair.

"You sure you're okay?"

She flicks my ear. "I'm *fine*—stop asking."

"Uh oh." I flip her over and start smacking her ass. "Sass will earn you more punishment."

She giggles. "I'm counting on it."

I slap her a few more times, then pin her wrists in the small of her back. "Here are the rules, little girl. No touching yourself until your next spanking. No matches. If you need to burn something, you come to me and ask for a punishment. No cock-teasing me at work. And no looking at the other guys." I smack her ass when she giggles. "I'm *serious*. Your second session will be next Wednesday." I lean over and kiss her blushing ass before I release her. "Go put your pants back on."

It's abrupt, but keeps us in character. If I'm honest with myself, I'd admit I'm not sure what we are out of character, and it scares me too much to examine. I need her out of here before I start turning into the sap I was with Samantha.

She rolls up, eyes still wide with wonder, like they were after I fucked her over on the table. She starts to walk past me, but I grab her waist and pull her back. "What do you say?"

I'm not sure if she'll slap my face after the way I dismissed her so abruptly, but she throws her arms around my neck and gives me a full kiss. "Thanks, Daddy," she breezes before she waltzes out of the bedroom.

My spent cock leaps back to life.

I don't know what the hell I'm doing here, but I'd better figure it out quick. Because this thing between the two of us is powerful.

CHAPTER 7

ia

WE'VE BEEN out on three calls already and I'm starving. We all hit the pasta like we're carbing up for a marathon and then head to our respective rooms to rest. My phone buzzes with a text.

My heart picks up speed when I see it's from Blaze. *I need you in my office immediately.*

Oh, hell yes.

I forget my exhaustion and post-meal sluggishness and swing my legs to the floor to stand. I open my door silently, but it seems Rocket and Scott never made it into their rooms, or they came back out. They're in the lounge, watching the Mateo Vega—aka The Matador—fight on television. He's a local favorite because the guy literally never gets hit. Not that I watch boxing, but I'm around guys who do all the time.

Anyway, their presence makes a visit to Blaze's office awkward.

His door is open, though, and I step inside it. His gaze shifts to behind me, and I hear footfalls but don't turn.

My brain clamors for something to say. "Uh, can I talk to you about the schedule?"

He pulls it out and slaps it on the desk. "Sure."

I walk toward him. As soon as I'm close enough, he murmurs, "Panty-check."

I sneak a glance over my shoulder. No one is there. I reach into my department-issued pants and pull up on the waistband of my new polka-dot panties to stretch the fabric. "One hundred percent cotton."

He eyes it like he wants to touch, but seems to hold himself back. "Good girl. You're dismissed."

I don't particularly like being dismissed. I don't know what else he could do—there are people in the lounge who saw me come in. But he's got me hot and bothered now, a slow pulse aching between my legs and no way to relieve it.

Plus, I can't stand the sting of rejection at being told I'm dismissed.

He did the same thing at his house the morning after my punishment session and I wasn't sure I liked it then, either. I guess he's making it clear we're not hanging out. We're not boyfriend-girlfriend. We're master and slave. Or daddy and doll. Or whatever name fits this kinky relationship.

And as much as I love what we're doing, how incredible the sex is, I'm not sure I can do sex without an emotional attachment.

I mean, is such thing even possible?

Maybe just for guys, I don't know.

I don't think it's me.

So I guess I need to talk to him.

Except do I want to break this thing off?

He suggested three punishments. It was a defined, finite thing.

When those are over, are we through? Should I at least get my three before I bail?

It's tempting. The last one was so incredible, I don't want to miss out on the rest.

I go back to my room and text him, *There are punishments for daddies who tease, too.*

His text comes through immediately. *Don't even think about it or you'll spend all day tomorrow sucking my cock.*

Then a second text follows. *Please say you'll delete both my texts right now.*

I laugh softly, but do as he asks. I know this forbidden relationship is dangerous for us both and I would never want to risk either of our careers. I text back, *done.*

Good girl, he texts back.

I'm starting to wonder about myself. About why those two words have such an effect on me. It seems supremely ironic after spending my entire life defying sexism to prove I'm capable of doing a man's job, I'd get off on being treated like a little girl.

At least four times since Tuesday night I've panicked, wondering what all this means about me. Am I flawed? How could I, of all people, want to be some guy's babygirl? How could I want to be disciplined and told what to do?

And yet I do. I just keep trying to remember this is sex. It's not real life. It doesn't mean I can't be a firefighter or that he doesn't respect me on the job… at least I hope it doesn't.

What if it does? What if I'm ruining my career because I couldn't help but get kinky with my captain? Because I sure as hell can't quit—I was lucky enough to get this position.

I jiggle my phone in my palm, staring at Blaze's name. Finally, I text something real, something bothering me. *Why does James hate me? Because I'm a woman?*

As soon as I do, I'm sorry. What's he going to say? You can't tell people how to make friends. They have to figure it out on their own. He's going to text not to worry about it, and I'm going to feel stupid for asking.

His reply comes after a moment. *You're replacing his cousin. He's still mourning that loss. Give him time.*

Oh. I suddenly feel like the biggest ass for not guessing it might be about the guy I'm replacing. I knew he'd been badly hurt on the job. I just was so caught up in trying to prove myself I forgot people might resent *anyone* who took his place—male or female.

I text back, *shit. I'm sorry.*

No, don't be. It's not your fault. He'll come around. They all will.

They all will. Does that mean the rest still haven't? I was kinda thinking I was part of the crew. I mean, I have a nickname and everything.

I hit the side of my phone to turn the screen off. Fatigue is making all this seem way more daunting than it should be. I reach for a book of matches. I thought about throwing them away after my first date with Blaze. I haven't lit one since. But now I'm glad I didn't. An addict never gets rid of their drug.

I need the flame. It will calm me down. Give me focus.

I rip off a match and hold it against the striking strip, but something won't let me flick it.

If you need to burn something, you come to me and ask for a punishment.

I want to, I really do. It actually sounds far more satisfying than lighting a match. Except we're at work. He can't give me what I need.

Still, I don't light it.

Instead, I flop back on the small bed and stare at the ceiling. After a minute, I stand up and grab the book of matches. I open my door and pad back out to Blaze's office.

He looks up at me, his blue eyes scanning my face like he knows something's wrong. I toss the book of matches on his desk.

"I need help." It nearly kills me to say it.

There's no smile on Blaze's face when he stands. He's dead serious, like I'm a fire he's going to put out.

And then the alarm sounds. Neither of us moves for a full three seconds.

I guess I'm not the fire.

"I'll get you after." His deep voice holds promise, rings like a vow.

I nod and we both move, running for our gear and the truck and the emergency we're trained to attack.

~

Blaze

IT'S ANOTHER ARSON FIRE. This time an abandoned building, a few blocks from the high school they burned last week.

Once again, Lia finds the evidence. She discovers three bottles of lighter fluid near an open window. I rode her ass last time for poking around after the fire is out, and I should've taken a bite out of her again, but I don't.

Mostly because a thought occurs to me.

Lia's good at this shit.

Why wouldn't she be? She's a pyro. She was the kid who played with fire. I'm almost certain she set the fire that burned her parents' house down, whether by accident or on purpose. So she knows how a pyro thinks. And, as if that wasn't enough, she's a cop's kid. All her family's in the NYPD.

It's like she was born to be a fire investigator.

It's a perfect profession for her.

I file that away for later, something to talk to her about—maybe research when the next training will be. It's not part of our department—fire marshals and fire inspectors are county positions, and we're city, but I know some inspectors. They usually come from our ranks—guys who have been injured or are getting too old for firefighting.

We climb back in the fire truck. It's two hours past our shift and we're all tired as shit, but I told Lia I'd take care of her, and I'm going to. The crew gets back to the station, and we strip off our turnouts and hit the showers. Lia's nowhere to be found when I come out, and I have to fight back a little panic.

She needed me and now she's gone off on her own.

But Lia's a big girl. She doesn't set fires or cause destruction anymore. She's not going to hurt herself or anyone else.

I could call or text her, but I'm too tired to navigate what to say. I don't even know if she still needs a release after the night we've had. I take the subway straight to her neighborhood and buzz her apartment.

She doesn't answer at first, so I buzz again in the 'shave and a haircut' rhythm so she knows it's a friendly 2 a.m. visitor. After a few more beats, her voice comes through the intercom. "Yeah?"

"It's me. Let me up."

She releases the lock on the door, and I go stomping up the steps. The door to her apartment is open a crack and I push right in.

Damn.

She's in her PJs, which consist of a tiny red cami and soft shorts that only cover half her ass.

I don't say a word. I don't know, I guess I've used my up my speaking quotient for the day. I wrap my fist in her hair and pull her head back. She blinks up at me, need and longing there, burning behind her eyes. My concern she no longer wants this evaporates.

I stamp my mouth over hers for a quick but brutal kiss, then walk her backward to her bedroom. I release her and unbuckle my belt. Her eyes track the movement, pupils dilating. I'm not going to use it on her—at least not the way she's thinking, but I love the flutter of her pulse in her neck. I pull her wrists behind her back and fasten my belt around them a few times before, pulling the end through the buckle.

I fold her over the edge of the bed, my dick getting chubby from manhandling her. The first swat is hard, but I rub the sting away, massaging as I relearn the curves of her ass. Her scent fills my nostrils, and a sense of satisfaction—of rightness pours through my veins. I slap her ass and once more rub it out. The sting of my palm brings my purpose into focus. Nothing matters but satisfying my little girl. Giving her everything she needs and more.

I pull her miniscule shorts off—time to get down to business.

I press one hand between her shoulder blades and start a proper spanking—hard, fast strokes meant to challenge her.

She gasps and twists, stamps her bare feet on the fluffy shag rug.

Seeing my handprints bloom on her flesh gets me rock hard. I keep spanking, steady and unforgiving, until she's panting and her ass is rosy pink.

Only then do I let myself touch between her legs.

Sopping wet. She's slick and swollen and begging to be taken.

It may seem backwards, but I can't take her without asking. Words need to be spoken now—it's time to untwist my tongue.

"What do you need, pretty girl?" My voice comes out sounding deep and gravelly.

"You." She answers without hesitation.

"You want my cock, baby?" I give it a hard squeeze through my jeans.

"Yes, Daddy."

My dick surges at her pet name for me. I scramble to pull out a condom and sheath myself before I rub at her entrance. She spreads her legs wider in invitation, but I have to stop and take in the picture she makes. She's fucking beautiful—my petite, lean-muscled fire warrior in the most submissive posture imaginable. Her small hands curl at her lower back, wide stance revealing the dew glistening between her legs.

I'm humbled by how willingly she gives herself to me—especially because I know it's not in character for her. Lia Burke doesn't roll over for anyone.

I ease into her, but the moment I'm engulfed in her wet heat, I lose all control. Thought vanishes. It's just my body and hers—a magnificent joining, the mutual giving and receiving. A humming of pleasure starts in my ears. Or am I making the sound with my throat? I don't know. All I know is I want to claim Lia in every way possible. I need more, even, than what we have. I want to be her man. Her daddy. Her everything.

I grasp her elbows to leverage into her harder and faster, my balls tightening for release.

"Fuck. Lia. *Fuck!*"

I come, forgetting to make sure she came first, but she's right with me, her tight channel squeezing my dick, making me lose my everloving mind.

Pleasure explodes and I fall forward, bracing my torso with my arms beside her on the bed. I bite her shoulder and her pussy contracts some more, milking more cum out of me.

"Beautiful girl," I murmur. "Nobody's ever made me come this hard."

"Me neither," she mumbles into the bedspread.

Remembering her position, I scramble to get off and unbuckle her wrists.

She doesn't move. I ease out and dispose of the condom.

She still doesn't move.

"Baby? You asleep already?"

She mumbles something incoherent.

I chuckle and scoop behind her knees to lift her onto the bed.

"I'm so tired," she murmurs against my neck.

"I know, little dragoness. Me too." I pull back the covers and settle her in the center of the bed.

She tugs me down with her. "You should stay. It's too late to go home."

I hadn't planned on staying, but she's right. I'm fuck-tired and now that I've come, my eyes will barely stay open. I kick off my jeans and flop down beside her, and I'm asleep in an instant.

~

Lia

I ADORE WAKING to the feel of Blaze beside me in bed. He's lying on his back, sleeping hard. There's something so satisfying about having a huge man in my bed. Not just any huge man—a freaking *stallion* of a man. And the guy who just barges in, ties me up and spanks my ass without saying one single word.

I kinda love him.

His cock twitches when I move in the bed, and I get a streak of naughty in me and reach for it. I put my hand inside his boxer briefs to fist around the base. He automatically pushes into my grip before his eyes even crack.

"That's dangerous." There's gravel in his voice and, like last night, no smile on him.

"Oh yeah?" I purr, sliding my fist up and down his length.

"Mmm." He pushes up to his elbows and runs a hand across his stubble. "Playin' with fire."

"I guess you know that's a habit for me." I cup his balls. A drop of pre-cum forms on his slit.

Now I see a twitch of his lips.

RENEE ROSE

"Gonna get yourself fucked hard, little girl." His growly warning makes my pussy squeeze and lift.

"What if I wanted to ride shotgun?" I ask, swinging a leg across his hips to straddle him.

His eyes grow dark, hands reach for my waist. "Is that what you want, little girl?"

"Is it an option?" My heart's increased in speed, like I'm testing boundaries here. Does he only do spanky sex? Does he always have to be in charge?

I'm too afraid to ask the real question that's been nagging me since we started this game—what does this all mean to him?

He drops his hand down over the side of the bed, like he's feeling for something. "Pretty hard to deny you anything." His hand returns with a condom.

My chest squeezes. This guy is too good to be true. I snag it from him and open it, rolling it over his thick member. I lift my hips up over him and lower myself onto his cock, taking him inch by inch. He's so big, it takes me a moment to adjust, but then I start rocking my hips slowly. His gaze grows heavy-lidded, traveling over my body with hunger. He grips my hips and starts pulling me over his cock.

"Ah, I see," I tease. "You let me lead for about fifteen seconds."

He shakes his head. "Fire," is the only word he says before he rolls and pins me beneath him.

I giggle as he wrestles my wrists down beside my head.

"Are you getting sassy with me, little girl?"

I buck my hips because he's not moving and I need more.

He pulls back and shoves in hard, like it's a punishment. "Hmm?"

"What are you going to do about it?" I dare, loving this game. My nipples are hard points, brushing against his chest, pussy pulses around his cock.

To my chagrin, he pulls out.

82

"Hey!" I sit up.

He pushes me back down and lifts my ankles in the air. I think he's going for the plow position for sex, but instead he starts spanking me.

Oh God. It's so delicious. The position pushes my lady parts out, so he slaps my pussy and my butt at the same time.

I buck, flexing my legs and reaching to cover, even though I love every minute of it.

"Are you gonna be good?" he rumbles.

I shake my head no.

A warm and affectionate smile creases his face. He kisses the inside of my ankle.

He grips the fronts of my thighs and slides me toward him, then shoves into me. Despite my caterwauling, I like it way better when he's on top.

He pounds into me, making sure I feel every muscle in his mammoth frame, every inch of his punishing cock. The bed slams against the wall over and over again, eliciting yells from the neighboring apartment.

I giggle and surrender, letting the sensations wash over me—pleasure mostly, a little pain.

It's great to let him lead. In this one small place in my life, I don't have to be perfect or in control. I don't have to prove myself. In fact, he likes me naughty.

He reaches down and pinches one nipple, hard.

I arch up with a cry.

He covers my mouth with his hand. He covers my nose for a second and I panic. He immediately releases my nose. "Hold your breath."

There's no question in his words. It's not a suggestion, only deep command, and I obey.

I hold my breath and watch him watching me. His brows are

drawn down in concentration as he plows into me without a break.

Urgency blooms within me— the need to breathe twines with the need to come, and I suddenly understand what he's doing.

The climax explodes out of me, stars dancing before my eyes. I suck in a breath as Blaze releases my mouth. I let out a wail of release as the bed dances against the wall, Blaze balling me with all he's got.

My wail rises in pitch and then he shouts, too, one hand flying to the wall above me while he fucks me through his release and more.

I float into another universe, knowing nothing but the rhythm of my breath matched with Blaze's, the mingled sweat of our bodies and the stillness in our sexual aftermath.

Blaze jerks, suddenly, pulling out. "What day is it?" he asks sharply. His eyes are on the clock beside my bed.

"Sunday."

"Shit." He climbs out of bed and starts pulling on his clothes. "I have to go. I have to help a friend move."

He shoves his boots on and clomps for the door. "Sorry to run out like this. I hope... ah... it was good for you."

I can't answer because I'm too surprised, too disappointed.

He waves before he's out the door and I pull a sheet up to cover myself, not that there's anyone to see me. Just because I've never felt so naked. I stare through my empty apartment, my heart pounding.

He hopes it was good for me?

What the hell does that mean?

Wow. I know exactly what it means. It means I'm a kinky hookup.

Blaze has a life—friends to see. Stuff to do. I actually know nothing about the guy other than that he's a captain at the fire station.

And why does it feel like he knows everything about me? Because I laid myself bare to him. Let him in, let him humble me.

I let things go way too fast. He was right about one thing—I was playing with fire.

And now it feels like I just got burned. No, not burned. I don't have enough information to know to what extent I've been used. Or how far he intends for this to go.

I've been singed, then.

I reach for a book of matches and turn it over in my hands. Striking matches really isn't that bad a habit. It's not like smoking, or drinking or cutting. It doesn't damage my body.

But the vision of my childhood home in flames flashes in front of my eyes.

I toss the matches on the bedside table. It's not because he told me not to.

It's because I'm stronger than this.

This is my choice.

CHAPTER 8

*laze*

THE TEAM IS out at the grocery store together, shopping for our shared meals when we get a call, which sucks. We leave our carts while Rocket promises the manager we'll be back and we jump in the truck.

The fire is another abandoned building.

"It's the same kid," Lia says with absolute conviction as she pulls up and lines up the truck with the hydrant.

"What makes you think it's a kid?"

She shrugs, already slipping out the door. "I just do," she shouts as she jogs to the back of the truck.

I get on with my job of assessing the situation and giving orders, and I don't have time to think of it again until I hear a shout and see Lia take off running—without a hose.

And then I see what she's running after. Or *who*, I should say.

It's a kid—you can tell by the slender limbs, although he's as tall as she is.

The teen, who'd been hiding around the corner of the building across the alley, sprints away.

Lia follows in hot pursuit.

Sonofabitch.

I run, too, because the only thought in my brain is the kid might have a weapon and she's going to get herself killed. Fear grips my throat.

Lia runs hard and fast, but the kid had quite a head start. He rounds the bend long before she does. I catch her before she rounds another bend.

"Get your ass back to the fire!" I snarl down the block. She's headed in that direction, but if she's still chasing the perp, I'm going to wring her neck.

Residents come out of their apartments and lean out of windows to gawk at the fire, and someone shouts something rude, mimicking me.

Lia nods and heads back toward the fire, so I retrace my steps down the alleyway, which is faster. Too much precious time has been wasted now.

Thank God the crew already has the hoses going and the flames out.

When we get back to the truck, Lia gets on the radio and tells dispatch to send the police.

I'm pissed as hell. I crowd her against the fire truck and pound my fist against it. "What in the *fuck* did you think you were doing?" I don't give her a chance to answer. I'm just warming up here— they do call me Blaze for a reason, and she's about to get the full brunt of her captain's temper. "You are not here to chase criminals —you are here to put out fires. When you abandon your crew, there are consequences to everyone. Someone could've been killed today because you decided to make up your own rules." I bang the fire truck again. I sense the rest of the crew behind me, but nothing's going to stop my tirade now.

"The fire was under con—"

"It's not up to you to make that call! I'm the fucking captain. I give the orders around here. If you don't like that, find another job. I need crew members I can trust to do what they're trained to do." Another fist to the truck. "Now are you willing to be a part of this team or aren't you?"

Too late, I realize Lia's eyes shine with tears. My tongue-lashing went way too far. I haven't had a female on the team before —didn't think to dial it back. I also didn't check my personal feelings for her. My anger boiled up over my fear for her safety, nothing else.

"Take a step back, Captain," Scott says in a low, calming voice and I realize, with horror, how threatening I must seem to Lia. I'm twice her size and while I'm not touching her, I have her backed against the truck. She doesn't look scared, though. Just angry and humiliated.

Fuck.

"I am," Lia mutters, lips trembling.

Now I'm pissed at myself for being the king asshole. I punch the truck again and walk away without another word.

The cops show up and I head over to brief them, even though it's really Lia's show.

"Don't worry about him," I hear James tell Lia. I guess if *he's* the first to console her, I really went too far. "He blows his stack sometimes, but everything's fine once he cools off."

I give my report as succinctly as possible, then call, "Burke!" to summon Lia.

She doesn't look at me when she walks over and I leave to give her space.

When she's done, I order, "Everybody in."

I don't ride shotgun because I imagine I'm the last guy Lia

wants to be sitting next to right now. I'll have to figure out how to fix this, and fast.

~

Lia

I AVOID Blaze the rest of the day. It isn't hard—he gives me wide berth. It's not that I'm mad at him—maybe I am, a little. I'm just scraped raw emotionally, and I can't look at the guy who put me there. I leave as soon as my shift is over and head home, my stomach still in knots over what went down.

He was right, of course. Running after the kid was rash and definitely not what I was supposed to be doing. Still, given a re-do, I'd probably do it all over again. I can't shake the feeling that the kid needs help. Maybe I'm just projecting my own self onto him, but I remember what it was like to start fires—to crave the destruction they cause.

I don't know why it's such a release, but it is.

And I'm fairly certain all three of these arson fires were set by that one kid. He needs help. Because if someone gets hurt, he's going to have to live with that for the rest of his life.

I change into a t-shirt and leggings and make myself a snack. When I'm done, I sit at my little two-person table with a book of matches in my hand. It's a new book—every match intact, lined up in two perfect rows. Just the sight of them releases endorphins. I fold one down, debating whether I'm actually going to tear it off. Whether I'll disobey Blaze and light it.

A knock sounds at my door. Probably my neighbor—it has to be a fellow resident, since no one buzzed to get in the main door. I open the door and then immediately swing it shut.

Blaze.

He thrusts his boot in the door to stop it from closing. "Hang on—just wait. I came to apologize."

I can't quite meet his gaze, although I feel its intensity. Instead, I stare at the hollow of his throat, at the stray chest hairs creeping above his collar.

"I'm sorry I yelled at you in front of everyone. I was an asshole. I didn't mean to humiliate you."

I don't move. I still don't meet his gaze, nor do I let him open the door any further.

"Let me in." There's no entreaty to his voice, only quiet command.

For some reason, I respond to this show of authority and drop back from the door.

He sweeps in, catching me up around the waist and walking me a few steps backward until I hit the wall. I push against his chest, but he catches my wrist and pins it to the wall beside my head. His mouth attacks mine in a searing kiss.

"Everything okay in there?"

Crap. Now it's my neighbor. Blaze came in so fast he didn't bother to close the door.

"Shut the door," he barks now, not looking away from me.

"Lia? Are you all right?" My middle-aged neighbor is a nice enough guy—a computer geek who takes care of his elderly mom. But now is not the moment for a visit.

"Yes, please shut the door," I answer.

Blaze rewards me with another brutal kiss. His thigh pushes between my legs, but when he comes up for air, he wants to talk. "You scared the shit out of me, Lia." He leans against his forearms on the wall, framing my head. "I thought you were going to get shot or worse. And then I just blew a gasket."

"I noticed," I mutter.

"I'm sorry I yelled."

It's way more of an apology than I expected, mainly because

everything he said to me was true. I don't know what to say, so I simply lift my lips for another kiss. He delivers, softer this time, although not gentle by any means. He slides a hand up my shirt and palms my breast while his tongue sweeps between my lips. I kiss him back, lifting one leg to wrap around him, offering no resistance as he helps pull it higher.

He shoves my bra cup down and thumbs across my taut nipple at the same time he bites my lower lip. "You ever been fucked up against a wall before?" He pulls my shirt off over my head.

"Uh uh." I unbuckle his belt.

"You're going to get it now." He whips his own t-shirt off and throws it on the floor beside mine. "Lifting that leg up around my waist. You're just begging to be fucked right here, aren't you, little dragon?"

I get his zipper down, but he catches both my wrists and lifts them up. "Interlace your hands and put them on top of your head."

I steal a glance at the harsh lines of his face as I slowly obey.

"That's right. Like you're under arrest. Now hold them there. You move, you'll be punished. Understand?"

I nod, my pussy clenching at the word *punished.*

"Good girl." He yanks my leggings down and off my legs. I wasn't wearing panties with them, so I'm standing in nothing but my tangled bra now. He taps my inner thighs. "Spread your legs." When I do, he squats down and licks into me, feasting on my juices.

I manage to keep my hands on my head for about ten seconds, but when he starts flicking my clit with his tongue, I forget all about the order. My hands drop to tear at his hair, pull his face into my pussy.

To my disappointment, he stands up, tsking.

Smack.

He slaps between my legs, spanking my pussy. "What did I tell you to do with your hands, Sparks?" I scramble to put them back on my head, but he shakes his. "Too late for that. Now you're getting spanked. I'll start here." He slaps between my legs again. It stings and I shift my hips, craving release.

He leans his forehead against mine and slaps me repeatedly between the legs. "You're going to get spanked hard, little girl."

"No," I whimper even though I love every second of it. I'm grateful for this reset—glad he's here, making me forget our quarrel.

"Turn around." Not giving me time to obey his order, he completes the action himself, spinning me around and pressing my hands against the wall. He pulls my hips so I'm forced to take a step back with both my feet. "Ass out, arch that back."

He slaps my ass.

I welcome the sting, the echo of flesh striking flesh that fills my small apartment. It's all I can do not to moan.

He slaps me again and again, gradually picking up speed and increasing intensity until I'm tucking my tail and dancing my hips away from his hand. "Turn around, Lia." His voice is rough, lips right beside my ear. I turn and he rolls a condom onto his length. He slides an arm behind my hips and lifts me. "Legs around my waist."

I love obeying him. In this scenario, anyway.

He lines his cock up with my entrance and eases in. One, two, three thrusts and he appears impatient with his inability to thrust hard. He carries me to the couch and lowers me, pulling out. He turns me around and bends me over the arm of the sofa, spanking me several times again before pushing in.

This time I don't hold back the moan. He gets so deep, the head of his cock rubbing my G-spot.

"Yes!" I cry out. He grips my hips and plows into me, his loins slapping my ass with each in-stroke, filling the room with the happy sound.

My pussy's embarrassingly sopping—wetter than I knew was possible. "Please!" I beg, not sure what I'm begging for.

"You need to come, baby?" His ragged voice seems both far away and inside my body.

"Yes! Please!"

He drags my hips back to meet his thrust and uses the moment to reach around the front. One rub of my clit and I come like a nuclear explosion—my consciousness shattering out to nothingness, my body knowing only pleasure, pleasure, pleasure.

Relief.

Joy.

Pleasure.

I forget who I am. Where we are. All the troubles of the day. I just *am*.

When I return to my body, I realize Blaze is stroking my back, his hips still pressed against my ass, his spent cock starting to slip out.

"I shouldn't be your boss, angel." Blaze sounds defeated. I don't move. He keeps smoothing his palm in long strokes up my back. "It's not fair to you. I'm going to lose my shit every time I think you're in danger."

I still don't move, don't speak. He's finally giving me something —even though it's just a breadcrumb—about how he feels about me. What I am to him. I notice he didn't say, "we shouldn't be doing this," which would be a more logical conclusion. But he's admitting he cares about me. And he's using the future tense—like we're going to keep being an item.

He pulls out and disposes of the condom, and I pick myself up from my prone position, reaching for my t-shirt.

He grabs it out of my hands as I start to pull it on. "I didn't say you could get dressed."

A smile tugs my lips despite the heaviness of the previous conversation. He winds the fabric around my back and uses it to tug me against him, his iron biceps caging me in. "Are you still mad at me?"

I shake my head. "I never was."

He arches a brow. "Yeah, you always slam the door in my face."

My lips twitch again. "Okay, I was a little peeved. But mostly I was just embarrassed and feeling awkward. I didn't want to look you in the face." My eyes slide away again now, as the sensation returns.

He cradles my head, his thumbs light on my cheeks. "Sparks, look at me." I lift my eyes to his. "I'm so sorry I came down on you in front of everyone. I lost my head and acted like a bully. I hope to hell I didn't scare you."

"I'm not afraid of you." It's true. Yeah, he was mad. He's huge and he backed me against the fire truck and banged his fist against the metal by my head, but I knew he'd never hurt me. Fear never entered the picture. I was just sorry I pissed him off.

Really sorry.

His brows dip. "I dragged you into the deep end with me real fast. We shouldn't even be hanging out together and here we are in this insanely hot and probably more than a little twisted relationship."

"Yeah." The word comes out breathy. "Well, I'm not quitting." I lift my chin in challenge.

Amusement dances in his eyes. "No surprise there, Sparks. Truth is? I don't want you gone. Maybe I should look into a transfer."

Shock makes my lips part. He would transfer away from his station for me? I don't want him to, but pleasure blooms as I realize he's that serious about me.

"I don't want you gone, either," I say quickly. "And you being boss kinda works for us, don't you think? Considering?"

His lips quirk, but then drop again. "Yeah, but look what happened today."

I consider the situation, trying to figure out what would've worked better. "So next time you want to reprimand me, you'll have to wait until we're in private."

Blaze opens and closes his mouth and then his eyes go dark. He attacks my lips in one of his signature blinding, searing kisses. "You're unbelievable, Lia Burke."

"Yeah?" I'm breathless and hot, my nipples tightening against his bare chest.

"Yeah." He stamps his lips over mine again, hands coasting down to cup my ass. "And you're all mine, aren't you?"

"Mmm hmm."

He bites my neck. "Say it."

I'm wet again. I lift onto my toes to rub my nipples over his hairy chest.

"*Say it.*"

"I'm yours, Blaze."

Another nip. "*Again.*"

"I'm yours."

"Damn straight," he murmurs, nipping and nuzzling my face, gentling. "You have plans tomorrow?"

I shake my head.

"Good," he says. "I want to spoil you." And with that, he picks me up and carries me to the bedroom, already ready for round two.

CHAPTER 9

laze

I HOLD Lia's hand as we walk to the subway. We just finished a CrossFit session together and I'm all horned up for her again, even though I fucked her twice last night and once this morning. CrossFit wouldn't have been my first idea for spoiling her on her day off, but she told me it would make her day if I came with, so how could I not?

Apparently she's not the fancy meal type. Or the spoil me at a spa. Not even a flowers and a movie kinda girl. No, this one likes to abuse her body while watching me work out beside her. I'm not sure who ogled who more.

Bottom line—I'm in love.

I'm smart enough not to tell Lia that. I know I'm moving too fast as it is, and I don't want to fuck this up.

But seriously? This girl is unbelievable.

Is it just about the kink? No. Yes. Maybe. I don't know. I mean, if she had told me this morning that she never wants to be spanked again, would I still want to see her?

Hell, yeah. I think she's amazing—smart, driven, adorable. Strong as anything.

But I wouldn't even know her if it weren't for the kink. I wouldn't have seen how willingly she surrenders, just drops her armor and lets me see her most vulnerable self. So yeah, it's all twisted together. But it's definitely way more than the sex.

We pass an ice cream stand and she tugs me toward it.

"You want some ice cream, little dragon?"

She spins in front of me and hangs on my arm. "Pleeeeease, Daddeeee?"

"Christ, you're getting me chubby. Why is that hot to me?"

She rubs her breasts against me. "Because you like to be in charge and I'm letting you."

She's right. The sense of power I get when she gives me control intoxicates me. With Samantha, I wanted to take care of her, but she never let me. She always pushed me away, even while using me to support her and her child, Lily. The little girl I thought of as my own until Samantha decided to bail and return to Lily's real dad. And she definitely wasn't into kink. Not even a little bit. The few times I tried to smack her ass, she told me I had issues.

Back then, I didn't know someone like Lia existed. Someone who not only lets me play out my dominant fantasies, but enjoys them as much as I do.

I propel Lia up to the ice cream cart and ask her what she wants. She orders a double scoop of chocolate and I get cookies and cream. She takes a long, seductive lick of her cone while holding my gaze.

I growl.

I have to bite my tongue to keep from demanding she move in with me. Today.

I need to slow way the hell down. And my first problem to solve is our work situation. The fire inspector idea might be the best possible solution. I just have to see if I can pull a few strings to make it happen...

CHAPTER 10

 ia

SECOND PUNISHMENT. I show up at Blaze's door in my attempt at a Catholic schoolgirl outfit. Lord knows, I wore one long enough, I ought to be able to put it together. My version tonight is white knee-high socks with a short blue skirt and a white blouse. Oh, and I might have put my hair in pigtails, too. I feel slightly stupid, but I'm hoping the look will pay off.

I'm starting to live for making Blaze horny.

I ring the bell downstairs, then climb up and knock on his door.

"Oh Jesus." He pulls me in and shuts the door. "That's so fucking cute. Will you wear that every time? Wait—" His brows slam down.

I've never heard so many words come out of Blaze's mouth so fast. Not counting when he's yelling.

"Second thought, I forbid you to ever wear that again. Did anyone fuck with you on the way here?"

I laugh. "No. And I can take care of myself."

He scrubs a hand across his face like he's deeply troubled over the thought of me walking here like this. "You'll leave the outfit here. Wear it for me alone. Got it?"

I laugh again.

He shakes his head. "I'm not fucking kidding. No one else gets to see this. Understand?"

Is it wrong that I love his jealous possessive thing so much?

He pinches my chin and lowers his face to mine. "I need a yes, sir."

"Yes, sir, Daddy."

He stares me down a moment longer, but I see satisfaction gleam in his gaze before he releases me. "Go to the bedroom, take everything off and kneel in the corner."

"Yes, Daddy," I say softly, dropping my purse on a chair as I head in. I strip out of my clothes. It was too soon to wax again, so I had to shave. It's not quite as baby smooth, but hopefully will still be as pleasing. I kneel in the corner.

This time everything seems familiar. I like the routine—it settles my nerves and helps me focus. I'm about to be punished.

I know it will be good, but it's still scary every time I surrender to Blaze. I always wonder if I'll hate it, or if it will be too much. Would I be too stubborn to use my safe word? Probably.

The door opens. I don't turn, just keep my face toward the corner, my heart thudding against my back.

"Come here, babygirl."

When I stand and turn, he's sitting on the edge of the bed, same as last time. Again, I'm grateful for the routine. I walk to him and he pulls me between his knees. He strokes up and down my sides, drinking in my body like I'm some kind of miracle.

"Are you ready for your spanking, Sparks?"

I nod. "Yes, sir."

"Good." He pulls me down over his thigh, my torso resting on the bed.

I settle into the spanking immediately. The first few slaps sting, but once I get used to it, I close my eyes and breathe, experiencing the slaps as only sensation, sometimes even pleasure. The heat grows between my legs as he swats my flesh. I don't count, but it seems to go on for a long time. Just when I'm starting to squeeze my cheeks together to avoid the pain, he stops.

"Good girl. You took that so well," he praises me. He rubs his fingers between my legs and I practically purr.

Yes, please, Mr. Daddy, sir.

Yeah, my thought-words are tumbling over each other.

He drags his fingers up the crack of my ass and massages my anus. I try to squeeze my cheeks together, but he delivers a sharp slap to each side. The snap of plastic reaches my ears, then he pries my cheeks apart and dribbles something cold on my crack.

I jerk my head up, peering over my shoulder.

"I have to get you ready for my cock, Sparks."

I turn my face back to the bed and bite my lip. I am seriously not sure I'm up for this. But it's Blaze, and I trust him, so I do my best to relax as he massages the lube into my anus, prying it open enough to fit his finger in.

I stifle a moan. It shouldn't feel good, but it does. I should be grossed out by this.

He removes his finger and replaces it with something cool and round. "Open for your plug, little girl."

I don't want to. I swear I don't, but my pussy swells open and I relax my anus when he pushes the plug against it. It stretches me open, wider, wider until I catch my breath and tense.

He stops and eases back, pumping with miniscule movements.

Oh God, it feels so good. So wrong. So very wrong. But so very good.

"Be a good girl and take your plug."

How can I not obey? I freakin' love when he calls me good girl. I concentrate on relaxing and he eases the plug in farther, farther, stretching me wide before it seats and the stretching sensation eases.

"That's it, baby. It's in. Now lie down on the middle of the bed, face up."

Thrills of excitement ping through me. The plug feels awesome —a constant but relatively subtle stimulus. I climb into the position he described and he buckles my wrists and ankles to cuffs attached to the bed.

What now?

"I think this is a very appropriate punishment, Sparks."

What is? Having my ass filled with a butt plug? It is rather humiliating, but I'm not sure why it's appropriate.

He walks to his dresser and picks something up. "You like to play with fire. I think you should experience a little burn."

Ah.

He returns with a lit candle.

My body lights up like it's seeing an old friend. I never thought of my pyromania as sexual, but in this moment, I'm so turned on by fire, I would orgasm with one touch. Blaze's smile is warm— there's nothing sadistic or frightening about his manner—not now, not ever. He stands over me and dribbles the wax on my belly. I jerk and shiver. My hips pop like I'm trying to fuck the air.

"You like that, don't you, my little pyro?" The bulge of his cock tents his jeans, letting me know just how exciting he finds this.

"Yes, Daddy." I want to beg him to touch me, but I also don't want this to be over. Everything about the scene is beautiful and deep. It cuts right to the heart of who I am. What I need.

He spills a little more wax on my nipple and I cry out, the heat scorching. When I realize he's watching my face intently, I nod. "It's okay," I whisper. "It's good."

"Is it?" He leans over and peels the flake of wax from my nipple to see the mark it left. He blows on the red splotch.

"It's okay. Please, Blaze. Go on."

He dribbles more, staying away from my breasts this time, concentrating on my belly, my thighs. Each drip is pure ecstasy—the initial scald, the quick cooling into a thrumming heat. He returns to my breasts, treats both to multiple dribbles of wax until I'm arching off the bed, straining at my bonds.

Then he moves to my pussy.

"Too late, I already waxed." My joke comes out shaky because I'm swollen with excitement. He releases wax right over my clit. It hits my labia and sears into the crack. "Ahh." My inner thighs shiver and clench, pussy and anus squeeze up tight. The sensation of the butt plug keeping my anus opens sends a second shudder through me.

Oh God, I really need to come.

I catch Blaze's eye. "Please, Daddy. I'm so ready. I'm on fire."

He squeezes his cock through his jeans. "Keep begging." His voice is deep and rough. "I fucking love it, Sparks."

I tug and pull at my bonds, wriggling and thrusting my hips. "Please, please, please?"

"You know where I'm going to fuck you, don't you, baby?"

Oh yeah. That.

But I need him between my legs, not in my ass. My pussy is a quivering, wet mess, dying to be claimed.

He walks over to his dresser again, returning this time with a vibrator.

Oh yes, please! I didn't realize I shouted it aloud.

Blaze chuckles and turns on the vibrator, stroking it over my slit like he's petting me.

"Oh please, just once more, please."

To my frustration, he shakes his head. "Not yet, little dragon. Your punishment isn't over until you've had your ass fucked. And I forbid you to come until after you've been thoroughly punished."

Oh lordy. That's so hot. My eyes roll back in my head and a full-body shudder runs through me.

He unclips my ankles and wrists. "Turn over, baby." I roll to my belly. He lifts my hips and shoves two pillows under them so my ass is high in the air. He spanks me—right cheek, left cheek, right, left, making the butt plug bounce and jostle, sending kicks of pleasure and urgency through me.

Another delicious prod with the vibrator over my sensitive bits.

"Reach back and hold your cheeks open for me."

Um, what?

His request is totally humiliating and yet it sends another giant wave of lust kicking through me. I do as he commands, my fingers cool against my heated ass.

He pumps the butt plug in and out of my ass a few times, and I start moaning like a porn star, but then he pulls it out. "I'm going to go slow, baby. You tell me if it's too much or you want more lube okay?"

"Okay." My voice sounds small. I sure as hell hope he's done this before. It definitely sounds like he has.

I hear the rip of a condom and the flip of the lube cap before I feel the slather of gel.

And then the punishment begins.

I'm bent over these pillows, holding my own ass open for the most humiliating form of discipline ever, and I love every second of it. His cock feels better than the plug—the velvet steel of his thick member stretches me wide again. He fills me, inch by inch. I moan and whine, my fingers twisting the covers of his bed.

It's too intense—more than I think I can take, but it's pleasurable, too. I don't want him to stop and yet I can't stand him going on.

I need... I need...

I shove my fingers underneath me. I have to touch myself.

Out of nowhere, the vibrator appears. Blaze shoves it into my fingers. I pull it down until it's right where I crave it, where I can grind over it.

And now I'm lost. I'm so far gone, I'm not just on another planet, I'm in another galaxy. All I know is the massive sensations that rock my body—the twin stimulations of anus and clit, the urgent fullness, the insane pleasure. I ride it, like I'm on a wave, out of control of my own body.

Blaze's thrusts get faster, harder.

I make a long, keening cry.

Blaze pulls back and retrieves the vibrator from me.

"No," I moan. "Please—I need it."

He finds the entrance to my pussy and fills me with it. Now I'm stuffed full—the vibrator and the cock vying for my attention. I'm going to shatter any moment now, just splinter into a million pieces. I can't take it. Too much. Too much pleasure. Too much sensation. Too much.

I scream.

Blaze pounds my ass four times and then shouts, burying his cock deep inside me.

My pussy spasms around the vibrator, and my anus attempts to contract around his thick cock, which makes me scream again. My body shakes and quakes as wave after wave of release roll through me.

Blaze is at my back, kissing my neck, murmuring things in my ear, but I barely notice. I'm too far away, too far gone.

"Blaze." I'm lost.

I find myself cradled in his strong arms as he croons something softly against my hair. I blink and focus on the lines of his rugged face. "Wow. Blaze."

"You okay, angel?"

"Mmm hmm. That was intense." I nuzzle into his chest, rest my cheek on his shoulder. My ass hurts—a burning in my anus that leaves me feeling well-used.

"You want a shower?" he asks.

"I don't think I can stand up," I admit with a shaky laugh. I'm slightly embarrassed now about how freaking intimate we just got. I feel like my packaging has been ripped open and my real self is spilling out all over him.

"I'll hold you, baby." He stands up from the bed, still cradling me like a baby and takes me into his bathroom. I'm not even sure how we get under the water, but Blaze doesn't put me down, he just holds me under the warm spray, rocking me gently.

I press my lips against his neck. "This is nice," I murmur.

"You were fucking amazing," he says, like anal sex is an Olympic sport. Actually, at this moment it feels like I just competed in an Olympic event.

And won the gold.

~

Blaze

I PUSH Lia up against the tile to get enough leverage to kiss her. She accepts my harsh kisses with a serenity that blows my mind. I love seeing her so wrung out like this.

By *me.*

I want to be the guy who leaves her limp and well-fucked every time.

I need more of Lia Burke.

All of her.

But right now my job is to take care of her, so I put her feet down and use a washcloth to gently clean between her legs and ass cheeks. I hold her up with an arm around her waist, because she still appears to be floating. I want to wash her hair, but I'm afraid she can't stand up without me holding on, and a one-handed wash isn't what I have in mind.

Next time.

Because I'm damn certain there's going to be a next time. A whole lifetime of next times, if I have my way.

CHAPTER 11

ia

I MOAN SOFTLY into the bedcovers. Blaze rolled me to my belly this morning, inspected my ass and then ordered me to spread my legs. Now, I'm lying boneless on his bed after he essentially fucked my brains out.

His phone beeps with a text and he picks it up and looks at it. Instantly, his shoulders tense and his mouth turns into a grim line. He glances at the clock and rolls out of bed.

"What is it?" I ask, even though it's none of my business. Or is it? I don't know. We haven't really defined our relationship.

"My ex. I have to get going. It's our daughter's birthday party today."

I sit up, my mouth turning bone dry, stomach knotting into a tight twist. "You have a daughter?"

"Yeah. Sort of. It's complicated. Listen, I'm sorry to run off. I didn't realize the time—not that I'm sorry about how we spent it, by any means." He gets dressed with the speed and efficiency of a firefighter.

"Your daughter's birthday," I echo again. I'm shocked by this information. I didn't know he had a daughter—or whatever complicated thing she may be. And the fact that he's not willing to explain it to me kind of tells me everything, doesn't it?

This isn't a relationship. He's not inviting me along to meet his daughter—not that I'm presuming we're at that stage, but still.

Or maybe I'm just bitter over him running off to his ex's while the bed's still warm from our love-making. Fucking. Whatever.

I get up, the bliss of my recent orgasm spiraling down into something dark and tired. I don't use any of my firefighter speed-dress skills. In fact, I move slower than usual, out of a wee bit of spite. I hate feeling like I'm being kicked out.

"You're welcome to stay here and sleep, if you want," he offers, somewhat mollifying me. Maybe he's hoping I'll still be here when he gets back. But then he adds, "I won't be back until late. I have to help a friend install some cabinets after the party."

"You're always helping someone, aren't you?" I try, unsuccessfully to keep my tone light.

He turns a shrewd glance at me and rubs the stubble on his face. "Yeah, it's a habit, I guess. Maybe it needs breaking."

I force myself to throw off my foul mood. "Nah, I think it's sweet. You like to be the hero. That's why you're the captain."

His smile seems forced, but I sail past him toward the door.

"Hold up." He sounds unhappy. He catches me around the waist and pulls me back against him. "Are you pissed?"

"No," I sigh. It's not really a lie. I'm not pissed, just disappointed. "I'm fine. Have fun at the party." I turn in his arms and offer my lips.

He gives me a perfunctory kiss, but his eyes still search my face for more information.

I don't give him the chance to sniff out my bad mood. It's just me being small, anyway. "See ya," I call and head out the door.

∼

Blaze

I SHOW up at the park near Samantha's with a My Little Pony and a stuffed rainbow unicorn under my arm. It's Lily's birthday. I couldn't possibly forget because the last time I watched her, she chatted about it non-stop. Turning four years old is a pretty exciting time.

I didn't think twice about coming, but now that I'm here, I'm wondering what the hell I'm doing. Lily's not my kid. She felt like my kid at one time. I saw her birth, I changed her diapers in the middle of the night, picked her up from daycare, watched her on my days off. Even now, Samantha still dumps her on me anytime she needs a sitter. Even though she doesn't deserve my help, I always do it because I freaking love her kid. I mean, I wanted to adopt her as my own when we were together.

Maybe it's because I just had Lia in my bed, but I suddenly question why Samantha and Lily are still in my life.

As a dozen princesses screech and race around the park, I stand there like a tool. Samantha ignores me from where she's chatting up the other moms. Lily's dad is nowhere to be seen, but that's not surprising. The guy's less than engaged with his daughter.

Maybe that's why I keep sticking around. I feel bad for Lily and the stupid choices her mother makes.

But no.

I don't wish I was still with Samantha and Lily. Not at all. In fact, I'm really fucking glad I'm not still carrying their weight. It was a whole lot of effort and responsibility without any thanks.

From Samantha.

Lily's always generous with preschooler hugs. She sees me now and comes racing over, throwing herself into the air. I catch her and swing her around, planting a kiss on her cheek.

"Hi, Mac," she says, using the name Samantha calls me by.

Samantha walks over and I set Lily down to run back to her friends.

"Hey. Can you go up to my apartment and carry the coolers down? They're super heavy." No hi. No please. Just another request.

This is nothing new and yet I'm seeing it through different eyes. I try to picture this scene with Lia instead of Samantha. Like if Lia and I had a kid together.

Whoa. That thought sends billows of warmth crowding out my chest.

Lia wouldn't be giving me orders. First of all, she'd be pulling her own weight because she's a hard-worker and doesn't shrink from shit jobs. But second of all, she's sweet and grateful. She lets me lead. She says thank you and sorry.

I turn and walk toward the apartment.

"You have a key?" Samantha calls. "Oh yeah, you do, right?" Yeah, I do. Because of all the times I've brought Lily home here and stayed with her after I put her to bed. Or when I had to stop by and pick up shit she was supposed to have at preschool. Or when Samantha called me to fix her leaking sink while she was at work.

Jesus. I'm a chump. When did I confuse my urge to take care of people with becoming a doormat?

I hold up my keys and keep going. I don't bother answering. Of course I'm not going to say no—I'm the only big guy here. But it's suddenly really fucking clear to me that I'm the chump being used.

I shouldn't even be here. Samantha and her boyfriend—Lily's

real dad—don't seem happy, but I don't give a shit about that. For the first time, I realize with absolute certainty that I would never get back with Samantha—not in a million years. I don't think I ever loved her in the first place. I *thought* I loved her. But I guess I was playing house. She was pregnant and needed a man, and I stepped in to be that guy. It felt good. I guess I like being the hero. Or the rescuer. It wasn't even about Samantha being the right one or what she could give to me. It was me seeking meaning by being a provider.

I carry the coolers out and help myself to a Sprite. As I stand there watching little girls run around, it's clear as day I don't need to be here. If I stopped showing up, Lily would forget me—hell, she would've already if I'd stepped back when I should have. Having me around may not be the best thing for the kid. It's probably confusing to her.

"Go run up and grab the cake, will you?" Samantha says.

"Nah," I say.

Her head jerks up in surprise and she frowns.

"I gotta go." I don't add *good to see you,* or *see you later,* because it's suddenly crystal clear that I'm done.

As I walk away, a twisted thought takes over me. Am I doing the same thing with Lia I did with Samantha? Just taking charge of her life, moving way too fast? Am I inventing a connection that's not there?

Sure, we like to have kinky sex—we're fucking awesome together. But I jumped right on her and attached myself like glue without even taking the time to know her. Did my domineering alpha male tactics sideline the chance for a real relationship?

Is that even what I want? Because if it is, I'm sure as hell going about it the wrong way.

Lia

I SPEND the late afternoon taking buses through our station's neighborhoods. I have a feeling our teen pyro isn't done, even though he came close to getting caught. I'm looking for likely targets in the same vicinity as the other two fires. By evening, I narrow it down to three empty buildings. One used to be a corner liquor store, another is an office building with the ground floor available for lease and the last one is an old Catholic church.

A little voice in my head keeps nagging me to stop this search, but I can't let it go. I want to help this kid. I take the bus back to the empty liquor store because if I were going to set a fire, it's the spot I would choose. It's on a corner without a ton of foot traffic, on a seedier street in the neighborhood.

My instincts pay off, because I see a slender figure skulking around. His dark bangs are long and hanging in his eyes and he wears that wary, ready to bolt tension in the angle of his elbows.

I walk on past because I don't really have a plan. Am I going to talk to him? What will I say—*Don't do it? The fire won't actually save you?*

That's what I want to tell him. But what are the chances of him listening? The kid needs help. And in order to get it for him, I'm best off catching him in the act. Then a social worker will get involved. He'll be in the system. Spoken like a cop's daughter, I suppose. I have faith in the system.

I round the corner and stop, my back against the wall. I wait as darkness presses in. My heart thuds against my chest, and I have to push away Blaze's warning about personal danger.

This kid is worth the effort. He needs help.

I pull out my phone, ready to call 911. Twenty minutes later I smell lighter fluid. I dial emergency and walk swiftly away so my voice won't be heard. "I'm calling to report an arson in progress.

314 W. Janey. Suspect is a dark-haired male youth, approximately five feet, 120 pounds." Being a cop's daughter means I know how to call in a crime.

"What is your name, ma'am?"

"Lia Burke, NYFD, off-duty."

"Is a fire truck required?"

"Not yet, but it will be if the police don't respond soon."

"Please hold on the line."

I drag in a long breath, forcing my heart rate to slow. "We have an officer five minutes away. Are you somewhere safe, ma'am?"

I look around the decrepit neighborhood. "No." Again, Blaze's anger with me over the last fire comes rushing back. I don't need to be stupid about this—I've done my part. I'm neither a cop nor on duty as a firefighter. "I am leaving the vicinity now. I'm available at this number for questioning or if they require a witness."

I hang up and walk swiftly toward a brighter street, where I catch a cab. On the way, I call Blaze. I don't know why—I just feel like he should know.

"Hey, Sparks," he answers. He sounds tired.

"Hey. I just saw the arsonist in action and I called the cops. I'm totally safe—in a cab on the way home."

Blaze is silent for a beat. I hope it's not his temper winding up.

"Jesus, Sparks," he finally exclaims. "Were you out looking for him?"

"Maybe."

He growls, but all he says is, "Can't get the cop out of you, can we?"

I might be imagining it, but I swear he sounds almost proud. It does something wild and fluttery to my pulse.

"Thanks for letting me know. And I'm glad you're safe. Something tells me you took a few risks, though, am I right?"

"Nothing I'll 'fess up to," I say with a note of finality to my voice. I may like his punishments over some things, but I don't want him to ruin this moment. I did something I feel good about. Maybe saved a building, but more importantly, I hope I helped that kid.

He seems to understand. "Well, good work, Sparks. You're something else, you know that?"

Again, the fluttery warmth spins around my chest. "So are you, Captain." I don't want to ask about the birthday party or his daughter, so I simply say, "Good night."

"Night, baby." His deep voice is warm and it sends ripples of warmth through my body as I end the call.

Blaze. He's an addiction. The man I can't get enough of.

But I have to be careful—there's way too much I don't know about him. Too much he's not sharing.

I need to guard my heart if I don't want to feel the same crushing disappointment I felt this morning every time he runs off to be a hero to someone else.

CHAPTER 12

*laze*

WE'RE the third company to arrive at an eight-alarm fire in Manhattan—some ritzy high-rise apartment with flames coming out the windows at the very top.

Lia parks Big Red at base behind the other two fire trucks and our crew pours out, each member doing his—*and her*—job.

The officer in command of the first crew briefs me. "Join staging on the eighteenth floor. The fire is on the top three floors and spreading. Ladder 54 is securing elevators and HVAC."

I bark orders for my crew to enter the building with their self contained breathing apparatus and start running in the hoses with nozzles and adaptors up the stairs. The pathway to the stairwell has already been marked in yellow fire tape and my crew takes the eighteen flights of stairs like champs. Once we reach staging, we're briefed on the situation. The fire has reached the twentieth floor and not all apartments have been checked for occupants.

Our company continues up the stairs to help get the fire under control, bringing our tools for forcible entry to get in the apartments. Black smoke thickens the hallway, heat seeping through our turnouts. Sprinklers are on, but they don't seem to have enough pressure. Hopefully one of the companies on the ground is working that problem out. We work our way through the apartments, breaking in and checking for occupants.

A dog's frantic bark pulls Lia toward the next apartment. She points toward it and I nod, helping her get the door open. The fire has consumed half the place, making it difficult to see. The dog runs toward us, but then stops, barking.

Lia squats down and pats her leg to call the dog, but it continues to bark, then run in a circle and bark again. Normally a dog would run out as fast at it can. Animals aren't stupid. If the dog won't leave, that means it's staying for something. Or someone.

I head toward it and it runs toward the fire.

Shit. Who's back there?

I push forward, Lia right behind me. The rest of our company follows in with the hose. I check under the bed—a common place for children to hide when there's a fire. Nothing.

That's when we see him. A kid no more than ten years old is slumped in a closet, his exit blocked by a caved in ceiling.

I start trying to haul the debris away to get to him, but Lia gets right down on the floor and army crawls underneath it, getting to the unconscious boy. She hooks an arm around his chest and drags him back the way she got in.

There's no way I could've fit through that gap—no way any of the other company members could have.

In this moment, I'm damn proud of Lia. Of my crew for having a woman on the team who can do things the rest of us can't.

My impulse is to help her up—to take the boy from her because I'm stronger, but I resist. Lia's working hard to prove herself, and I'd be the biggest ass if I took this moment from her.

Instead, I let her scramble up and carry the kid out, the loyal dog right on her heels, protecting his charge.

∼

Lia

THE NEWS CAMERAS catch me emerging with the boy and dog. Later, when the fire is out, they get my name and ask me questions about how long I've been on the squad and what it's like to be the only woman.

Knowing this is PR for the whole department, I keep it one hundred percent upbeat and positive. We just put out a fire in Manhattan—these people might be the kind who want to donate to our fundraisers.

To my utter humiliation, the whole crew watches the evening news at the station over a spaghetti dinner. There I am—covered in soot and looking almost as small as the boy I have slung over my shoulder.

Then they cut to me with my helmet and SCBA off. "So what's it like to be the only woman on your crew?"

I sound like a politician running for mayor. "It's an absolute honor. I've wanted to be a firefighter my whole life and working with these guys is a dream come true."

Rocket leaps from his seat, affecting a fairytale princess pose and using a high-pitched voice. "I just love working with the dreamy guys at Ladder 61!" he mimics.

"Shut up." I throw my balled up napkin at him.

Blaze's face comes on the T.V. and I turn back to listen.

"What's it like having a woman on the crew, Captain?"

My stomach tightens. I'm embarrassed to be watching this in front of everyone. Embarrassed to be talked about on T.V.

The Blaze on camera appears annoyed by the question. "You know, I wasn't sure how it would work out at first. I mean, I knew she could do the job, but I didn't know how it would change our team dynamics. But I have to say, she brings something to the crew we didn't have before. That kid she saved was caught in a tight place. She was the only one small enough to crawl through and get him. If she wasn't on our team, it might've been too late by the time we cleared the path."

I drop my eyes to my spaghetti and blink back tears. I saved a kid today. It's the first time it's hit me. I'm living my dream—saving lives. I have to fight back the disconcerting sensation that I'm going to start bawling like a baby.

"Eight years I've been fighting fires and I've never been on television. Guess I need a set of tits," James mutters.

The urge to cry evaporates. I lift my eyes to James, but he won't look at me.

Rocket shovels a bite of spaghetti into his face and talks with his mouth full. "Duh. She's a helluva lot prettier than you, asshole. You think they want to put your ugly mug on T.V.?"

"Well, they put on the captain's," Scott points out. "And he's the meanest and ugliest of all of us."

Blaze grunts and stands, dropping his dish in the sink before walking out.

He's a man of few words around here, which normally makes me giddy when I think about how expressive he is when we're alone, but since Sunday, only makes me uneasy. I still don't know anything about his daughter or his history.

I stand up and clear the dishes. I'm on dish duty again, but Scott helps me.

"So how's it feel?" he asks, taking a wet dish from me and drying it.

"What?"

"Saving a life."

I draw in a breath, not even sure how to label all the emotions swirling around me. "Humbling," is the one I finally pick.

"Yeah, humbling—I agree." He takes another dish. "A million times better than when you fail to save someone."

I stop washing dishes for a moment, the weight of his words pressing in on me.

"God, I'm not prepared for that inevitability," I confess.

"Yeah, you never are. No matter how many times it's happened. Blaze takes it the worst of any of us. He's got a rescuer complex, you know?"

My scalp starts to tingle with some awareness I don't want to have.

"Yeah, I'll bet," I manage to say.

"Once we were putting out this fire. The neighbors were yelling that there were kids in there. We went in through the upstairs window." He just shakes his head, like he can't go on.

I don't want to ask, but I still do. "It was too late?"

"Yeah. Six kids. All lying there on the floor. Blaze didn't speak for two weeks."

"Does he—" I swallow. I both want and don't want this infor- mation. "He has kids of his own?"

Scott makes a dismissive sound. "Not really. The kid isn't his. That was another rescue mission of sorts. He started dating this pregnant woman. He supported her through the whole thing—coached her through the birth, stayed up all night with the crying baby, changed diapers, took care of the little girl on his days off. He played full-on daddy to that little girl. And then when things get easier and the kid is a preschooler, the bitch dumps him and goes back to the baby-daddy."

I want to hurl my dinner. The story is upsetting on more than one level. To think of strong, solid Blaze getting used hurts. But I can't stop my brain from stuttering on the words *another rescue mission.*

Is that what I am to him?

The thought nauseates me. Everything that had been sexy and fun becomes a dark, twisted mess. Am I a project for Blaze? A girl crying for help?

How could I ever let myself be so debased? Me—the tough girl.

~

Blaze

I HANG up the phone and tap my pen on the station desk. It's done. I've arranged for Lia to take a leave of absence for a certification course in fire forensics.

When I called the battalion chief a couple days ago, I was certain it was a good idea, but now, after Lily's birthday party, I'm having misgivings. Am I getting too involved again? Diving into someone else's life and making it my own?

What if she thinks I'm too controlling, too involved, just too *much* like Samantha accused me of being?

And it pisses me off I'm even thinking about Samantha. She was a mistake.

Lia's different.

At least I think she is.

But will she see my attempt to support her as interference?

I sigh. There's only one way to find out. It's almost the end of our shift and I need to post the upcoming work shifts.

I pick up the schedule for the next two weeks and pin it up in the hallway just outside the office door. "Schedule's posted," I yell to no one in particular.

Rocket, Scott and Lia wander out.

I take refuge behind my desk, bracing myself, waiting for the inevitable question. Fuck, I should've talked to Lia about this plan privately first. How will I mention my plan that she move in with me while she's training?

What was I thinking?

Sure enough, her ponytail whips as she whirls to look at me, hands on her hips. "Why am I off the schedule?"

I clear my throat and stand up from the desk. In my mind, this was going to be an awesome moment where I make up for being a dick and yelling at her in front of everyone by now praising her in front of the crew. But judging by the way her eyes flash, she's not exactly receptive.

She's already jumped to some erroneous conclusion.

Still, I go for jaunty. "Sparks, you've been selected for a special training." I really wish the other fucks weren't standing around listening.

She arches a suspicious brow. "Oh yeah? What's that?"

"Fire inspector certification." I try to sound detached and professional. "Your interest in detective work at the site of fires has been noted, and the department agreed to give you a leave of absence while you complete the training."

Lia's jaw drops. But not in a good way. In fact, I'm pretty sure there are flames coming out of her ears. *"What?"*

Shit. I totally screwed the pooch with this one. I go ahead and drop the rest of it on her before she explodes.

"Training starts next week, but you're off the schedule for the rest of this week to job shadow with Inspector Patton."

She shakes her head slowly. "No."

Okay. This wasn't the response I expected. When I cooked up this plan, I was definitely going to be her hero.

I rub my jaw. "Listen, maybe I overstepped—"

"Ya *think?*"

I glare at Scott and Rocket, but neither of them show any intention of moving along. I turn back to Lia. "I believe you have a real talent with this stuff. I had to pull a lot of strings to get it all arranged."

Wrong thing to say.

"No one asked you to pull strings. In fact, I didn't ask to be a fire inspector at all. I guess that speech you gave the reporter today was total bullshit. You don't think having a woman on the team is a good thing. You want me safe and sound, away from danger. Isn't that right?"

Sonofabitch. "Lia, that's not why—"

"Yeah, right. You know what, Captain? Save it." She turns to survey the rest of the crew. "I heard you assholes were taking bets on how long I'd last. Well, this was one sneaky bitch of a way to get rid of me, wasn't it? Make it seem like I've won the freaking lottery. Well, thanks. Thanks a whole lot."

She grabs the schedule from the wall and crumples it up in her hand as she stalks out.

Fuck.

"Lia, wait." I jog after her. I don't care now who sees us together or what they think. I just need to talk to her. "It's not like that. Will you just wait?"

She heads out the door and jogs down the steps, flipping me the bird over her shoulder without turning.

Shit.

Fuck, fuck, fuck.

I stop pursuing her. Maybe it's better to let her cool off first, then I can explain.

Damn.

~

Lia

BLAZE HAS ALREADY LEFT five texts by the time I get home. I'm too pissed to even look at them. I'm also too pissed to do anything but stomp around my apartment. Eating and sleeping seem like an impossibility.

My phone rings.

I know who it will be. Fuck it—I answer. "You have some nerve, you know?"

"Lia." Blaze sounds relieved. "Will you please just let me explain?"

"Okay, yeah. I'd like to hear how you explain this. Go ahead."

"First of all, I'm not trying to get rid of you. No one is trying to get rid of you. That's not it at all. I honestly think fire inspector suits your skill set."

"Oh, what skill set is that?" My voice drips with lethal sarcasm. "Setting fires?"

He draws a breath and I know I've hit the nail on the head.

"Great. Thanks. You know—I get it. You're a fixer. You like to help people. You act like a grump but you're actually the guy everyone calls when they need a hero. And I became your new project. The pyro who can't get over her guilt. You saw my problem straight away and you stepped in to fix it." My voice breaks, the pain of what I'm saying tearing me in two. Because as I speak the words, I know without any doubt, every word is true.

"Well, thanks but no thanks. I don't need fixing." My eyes smart and my nose burns. "I'm not broken. And even if I were, I can take care of myself."

I hang up on Blaze before he can reply.

Because really? What can he possibly say? I know I'm right.

He calls back but I block his number.

I don't need to hear his shit.

I open the kitchen drawer and pull out a book of matches reflexively, but of course I remember Blaze's attempt to cure me of this. I crumple the matchbook in my fist and hurl it at the wall.

Fuck him.

I don't need his help, or anyone else's. I don't have a problem.

There's nothing wrong with me.

And if that means walking away from a fire career to prove it, I will.

~

Blaze

I PUNCH the wall in my living room.

Sonofabitch.

How could I fuck something up so badly?

Something that actually means something to me. *Someone* who actually means something to me.

Lia isn't a rescue project. She's the only bright spot in my life. Why didn't I realize that sooner and show her? Tell her?

Why in the fuck do I always have to be a hero? What made me think I could 'fix' things for Lia? I was trying to help, but I did it in the worst possible way. I should've talked to her, offered my help—which she probably wouldn't have accepted. I guess that's why I went around behind her back. It wasn't just to surprise her. It was to railroad her.

And that makes me a goddamn asshole.

I suck at relationships. I should've learned from my experience with Samantha. I'm too controlling, I jump in too fast. I try to make something out of nothing.

Clearly that's what I did with Lia, too.

And if I care about her, I need to back the fuck off. She doesn't want my help. The best thing I can do is leave her the fuck alone.

I punch the wall again, satisfied when the plaster crunches and my knuckles come away swollen and torn.

And then I whale on that wall with both fists until the entire panel is in a crumbled heap at my feet.

CHAPTER 13

THE TROUBLE with anger is that when it goes away, there's often a worse feeling underneath. Anger hides the true emotion. Often it's fear, like when I bluster and bluff my way through things.

Right now it's heartache.

Because breaking up with Blaze is the worst thing I've done.

That's not true. Burning down the house was the worst thing. But splitting with Blaze comes in as a close second.

My heart is a sunken stone, far below my solar plexus, but not quite to my bowels. It's sloshing around in my stomach, making it impossible for me to eat. Or walk. Or move really.

Which is why I spent the past three days in bed.

The guys from CrossFit texted to find out why I no-showed— because I never no-show unless I'm on shift.

The worst of it? Today's my birthday.

Worst birthday of my life.

I have to drag myself out of this bed and get to my parents' house, but eating my mom's home-cooked food and listening to the banter of my overbearing family is the last thing I want to do.

I should tell them I got called in to cover a shift.

No, my mom would just insist on rescheduling for tomorrow.

My phone rings. I check the screen. It's my cousin, Talia. She's probably the only person in the world I would answer the phone for right now. I swipe my screen. "Hey, girl."

"Happy birthday to you, happy birthday to you—"

"Yeah, thanks." I cut in before she can finish singing the whole damn song.

She must catch the heaviness in my tone, because she immediately drops the chipper thing. "What's wrong?"

"Ugh," is all I can say.

"Is that a guy-related *ugh* or a job-related *ugh*?"

"Kinda both."

"So a captain-related *ugh*."

"You nailed it."

"What happened?"

"Well, the douche took me off the schedule and signed me up for a two-month training to become a fire inspector—without asking."

"Okaaaay." My cousin draws out the last syllable, like she's not sure what my problem is. Well, of course she doesn't. Because she's missing some key information. Information I wasn't planning on sharing. Except I really need a friend right now.

"Here's the thing. He signed me up because he thinks I have a problem. With fire. He's been trying to fix me this whole time. I don't even know if we were really dating. I mean we were having crazy kinky sex but—"

"But what?" she prompts when I stop.

"But it was like... punishment sex. Kinky shit. He offered to help me, um..." I break off, unsure how to go on. "Talia, I have to tell you something." My voice breaks. "Something awful. Something I did that's really unforgivable."

"Okay, honey. Just tell me. Say it fast and get it over with."

"I set the fire that burned my family's house down."

I hear her exhale through the phone, but her words stun me. "I know."

My heartbeat seems to echo off the walls. Blood rushes in my ears. "You... know?"

"Everyone knows. You were always funky with matches. Squirreling them away. Lighting them in your room. It was an accident, though. Right? You didn't purposely—"

"Of course I didn't!" I interrupt. My brain in still stuttering on her words. "What do you mean everyone knows?"

"I don't know, it was sort of one of those family agreements to never mention it to you, because you probably felt bad enough. No one wanted you to think you were responsible for the house burning down. Even though the fire inspector found the fire started in your garbage can."

I don't realize I'm crying until tears drip down my chin. "They did?" I ask through my tight throat.

"It's okay, Lia. No one blames you. But what does this have to do with your captain? You told him and now he wants you to be a fire inspector?"

I sniff and swipe at the tears on my face with the back of my hand. "Basically, yes. He knows about the fire and he knew I felt guilty. So he's been..."

"He's been what?"

"Punishing me." This is really fucking embarrassing.

"Oh. Wow. That *is* kinky. Did you like it?"

"Um, yeah. Definitely. But then he signed me up for this job. And I found out about his last girlfriend—he jumped in to be her birth coach and the surrogate father to her baby. You see? He has a rescuer complex. And I'm just another project to be fixed."

"Yeah, I see. That sucks. So did you tell him to back off?"

"I told him to get lost."

Talia goes silent for a moment. I switch the phone from one ear to the other, then back again. "And now you miss him?"

Damn. How does she always get this shit right?

"I don't know," I lie. "I mean, it's not like we had anything worth hanging onto, right?"

"Hmm. That sounds like your head talking. But I'm guessing your heart says something different."

Said organ gives a squeeze, as if to prove her right.

"Well, let's talk this through. I mean, you liked some of it. You liked the kinky sex. You didn't mind him fixing you when he was doling out your punishment, right?"

My heart picks up speed at the truth of her words. "Yeah."

"But he overstepped with the job thing. Was that as a boss or as a boyfriend?"

I rub my ear. "Not sure. Both, I guess."

"Does that interest you?"

"Maybe," I admit. "But he should've asked."

"No question there," Talia assures me. "Are you going to go do the training? When is it?"

"Next week. And yeah, I guess. I mean, Blaze took me off the schedule, anyway. I don't know how he thinks I'm going to pay the rent." Except deep down I'm quite sure Blaze would've come to my rescue on that, too. And he would've enjoyed it.

And this time, the thought doesn't piss me off. It just makes my chest ache. Whether it's for Blaze or myself, I'm not sure.

Blaze

"I CAN'T HELP THIS TIME," I snarl into the phone and end the call. Everyone and his brother wants me to help them move. This time it was Scott, who is helping out some friend I've never met.

Fuck that shit.

Lia was right. I have a savior complex. Correction: I *had* a savior complex. No more. I'm over it. I don't need to equate my self-worth to being everyone's knight in shining armor.

Putting out fires is enough. I don't need to rescue Samantha, or my parents, or my neighbors or my co-workers' friends.

Lia is another story.

I do still want to be her knight.

Is that totally wrong? I guess it is.

I've been wracking my brain trying to figure out how to fix this. I definitely thought I was doing what was best for Lia. I still do. But I also pushed my own agenda because it conveniently solved a couple of my own issues—namely, the illegal nature of our relationship, and me worrying for her safety.

I called Inspector Patton to report Lia wasn't feeling well and asked to reschedule the job shadowing. I haven't cancelled her training for fire inspector, but I can. I'll lose half the fee, but I don't give a shit about that. But none of that solves my real dilemma. How to win Lia back.

Because despite my resolve to back down and give her space, to stay out of her life if she wants, I *can't*.

I'm not giving up yet.

So now I have to figure out how to get a second chance. How to get a face-to-face to apologize. How to convince her I won't steamroll her life again.

But what if I do?

Damn, that thought keeps gutting me. What if she is better off without me?

No.

She couldn't have faked what we had in bed. And clarity comes seeping in.

That's where I went wrong. I took something that she enjoyed sexually—being submissive, calling me daddy, letting me call the shots—and I took it out of the bedroom. Into real life. And in doing so, I stripped her of her dignity.

And the worst part is it made her question my motives for everything. She thinks I see her as less-than, when she's anything but.

But how do I get her to see it's not true? Just telling her won't be enough. She has to believe it.

CHAPTER 14

 ia

I SHOW UP AT MY PARENTS' house with a pasted on smile, even though I can barely put one foot in front of the other. It's hard to believe breaking up with a guy I wasn't even sure I was dating can hurt this badly. I just keep seeing Blaze's tortured expression when I got mad, keep wondering how he's taking all this. For some reason, I have a ridiculous need to know he's all right.

That he's not suffering.

Which is stupid.

Wouldn't I want him to suffer for taking me on like a social work case?

But no. I definitely don't.

The house is a loud clatter of voices and activity, as always. I do the round of greetings like a robot running a program. But I can't pretend anymore. When we sit down around the giant table to eat —adults inside, kids at card tables outside—I clear my throat. "I'm sorry."

"For what, *mi amor?*" my mom asks.

"For burning the house down."

The noisy dining room goes dead quiet, all the side conversations silencing, all eyes turned to me.

"Talia told me that everyone knows." I look around the room, find the eyes of each of my brothers, of my mom, and finally, my dad. "So, I wanted to tell you how sorry I am." I choke up on the last word and then everyone moves, everyone speaks at the same time.

Hands drop on my shoulders from either side. Words come at me. *It wasn't your fault. You were just a kid. It was an accident,* reach my ears.

I blink back tears and nod. "Well, I'm still sorry. That's all."

"Nobody ever held it against you," my father says from across the table, tipping his beer bottle in my direction. "Nobody." He says the last word fiercely, like he's daring me to disagree.

"You always were so fascinated by fire," my mom says. "And now look at you—we couldn't be more proud. You put your interest to work in the best possible way, didn't you?"

That's what I had always thought, but I'm suddenly not so sure. Was I just doing it for my family? To make up for my horrific crime and my cowardice about not telling them? And to think they knew all along!

I sniff. "My captain thinks I should become a fire inspector."

My brother Alex lowers his fork. "That's not a bad idea, sis."

I shrug, too mixed up to know if it's a good idea or not.

"You'd be a detective, like me." He grins and winks at me, and I can't help but feel a small tingle of pleasure at hearing how proud he sounds of me.

"Well, there's no telling if I can get a job as one. Look how long it took me to get onto the FDNY. But I might take a training for it."

"You should," Alex says, his expression still glowing with enthusiasm. "I think that's a great idea. So your captain—he must really see your potential."

My heart stutters to a stop, then reboots with a thunk. Does Blaze see my potential? Or was he just trying to get me off the crew, somewhere safe. Or out from under him so we can date.

Neither of those motivations would be reason to vilify Blaze, though, would they? They show he cares.

He cared enough to pull strings and make arrangements for me.

He shouldn't have done it without asking, but he did act with my best interest in mind.

Tears pop into my eyes again and I blink them back. "Yeah, he's a good guy," I manage to say, probably not pulling off casual as well as I hope.

Blaze is a good guy. He's a great guy.

And I probably owe him a chance to explain himself. I'll send him a text when I head home to open the door for a talk.

~

Blaze

I WAIT outside Lia's apartment for ninety minutes before I see someone approach. I'm not sure if it's lucky or unlucky that I recognize the guy. He's the geeky neighbor who asked if she was okay that night I left the door open.

"Excuse me—hang on!" I call out, jogging up to him.

He flinches and throws me a suspicious look over his shoulder, but the flowers catch his eye and he stops. "Hey, you live next to

Lia, right?" I speak fast before he pushes in and leaves me with my dick hanging in the wind. "Today's her birthday and I wanted to leave this for her. Could you let me up? Or will you leave these in front of her door for me?"

He gives me another guarded sweep of his eyes, but snatches the vase with the giant bundle of flame-colored flowers from my hand.

"This too." I thrust an envelope forward. It's my apology and the outline of how I hope to fix the situation.

The neighbor gives it a mistrustful glance, and I draw up just a bit, using my size now to intimidate him. He grabs it and pushes in.

"Thanks, man!" I call after him and return to my park bench where I can keep an eye out for Lia's return. I've never felt more like a stalker. I think about leaving about twenty times. But it's too late now—the note went upstairs. She'll be looking out her window. If she reads it.

I guess the chance of her chucking it straight in the wastebasket is medium to high.

When I finally see her approach, my chest cinches up tight. There's no spring in her step. Her youthful face appears older, and tired. Dark circles are under her eyes.

Shit. I did this to her.

I don't get off the bench until she's inside. I'm not going to force my presence on her until she's ready to talk. I need to give her space. But I also need her to know I'm going to do everything in my power to make things right.

I pick up the paper bag of lighter fluid beside me and get to work.

It's showtime.

~

Lia

WHEN I GET to my door, I find a giant vase of flowers propped against my door. The flowers are spectacular—like nothing I've ever seen. Brilliant flame-orange tiger lilies mixed with blood-red roses.

It's a fire bouquet. The flowers you give to a pyro.

My foolish heart picks up speed, thrilled to be honored this way. I pick them up and find a long envelope behind with my name scrawled on the front in block letters. I open the door and stumble in, setting the flowers down to tear open the envelope.

Lia,

You were never a project to me. You were (are) the brightest thing to come into my life in a long time. Maybe ever. I think we had (have) something special together, and I sure as hell am going to do everything in my power to get it back.

I'm so fucking sorry I tried to dick with your life without talking to you first. I never should've presumed that way. I understand now that I took the dynamic we have in the bedroom and applied it to real life and that was wrong and offensive.

I want you to know that I put you back on the schedule starting tomorrow, and I got myself transferred to another station, so you don't have to worry about anything being awkward when you go back to work.

That doesn't mean I don't want to work this thing out with you—I definitely do. I'm going to do everything I can to prove how much I respect you as a person, a firefighter and the woman who turned my world on its head in bed.

But I know I tend to move too fast and smother, so I want to give you space and time. That's why I'm saying this in a letter and not crowding you in person.

Lastly, I want to say I don't need to fix you. There's nothing wrong—

you're perfect as you are. In fact, I want to honor and love everything you love—including fire.

Please look out your bedroom window.

MY BREATH SUCKS in and I'm already running to my bedroom and pulling open the shade.

I spot Blaze below, standing in the middle of the street, facing my window. As soon as he sees me, he strikes a match and drops it into the street.

I cover my mouth with my hand, choking on a cry.

There, in the middle of the dark, empty road, is a fire. Not just any fire—flaming words: *I [giant heart] U Lia.*

My vision blurs as I watch the flames curl and lick and then die out.

Blaze holds up a finger. Uses a bottle of lighter fluid to write something else and throws another match down.

Sorry, it says.

"Hey you!" One of my downstairs neighbors leans out her window. I can hear everything through the single glass pane windows in this old building. "What do you think you're doing? I'm calling the cops!"

I throw my window open. "It's okay!" I open my window and yell down. "He's with the FDNY. He can put it out."

Blaze straightens and pulls the hem of his FDNY shirt down to display the big white logo scrawled across his massive chest. Then he turns back to me and holds up his finger one more time.

He writes again. This time:

Happy Birthday.

I pull my head back out of the window because I don't want him to see me cry. Somehow this has turned into the worst and best birthday of my life.

When the flames extinguish, all he does is lift a hand in my direction and walk away.

He meant it about giving me space.

I can't help but notice the gaping hole left in my chest cavity where my heart used to be. Space from Blaze feels all wrong.

So does working at the station without him.

I hate his solution.

I shut my window but stay there, forehead pressed against the glass, remembering the beautiful flames shaping my name.

He loves me.

He said so.

And how could I not believe it? He's willing to leave his station and his crew.

For me.

And he's not making my pyromania wrong—he gave me gifts of fire. I laugh, suddenly realizing how fabulous it is for a fire-junkie like me to end up with a guy named Blaze. It's like fate drew us together.

ia

I LITERALLY CAN'T STAND BEING at work without Blaze. Especially knowing it's my fault he's gone.

The rest of the crew is as freaked out as well. No one knew his absence was coming, and everyone wants to know what the hell is going on. Especially because the new captain is a doofus.

I mean, he's fine. Whatever. He's just not Blaze.

"Captain MacKenzie and I swapped stations," Captain Elmore tells us when we all show up. "He's over at the 151st and I'm here with you all."

"Well, *why?*" James demands.

Elmore says, "Personal reasons," and trucks off for the office.

"What the fuck does that mean?" Rocket says.

I spin around and head to my room without saying anything,

but I don't last long there. Everything about this firehouse makes me ache for Blaze.

I find my way back out to the hallway where Rocket, Scott and James are still standing, discussing Blaze's absence. "It's because of me," I blurt. My cheeks heat when they all stop talking and stare at me. "We, um... got involved and he figured it wasn't a good idea for us to work together."

If I thought they weren't sure they wanted me on the team before, it's clear now. Their looks make me want to sink into the ground and stay there.

I swallow. "But, um, I'm going to leave so he can come back. This is his station. He shouldn't have to leave it."

The guys still stare at me like I have five heads and some Medusa-like snakes spinning from them.

"Bullshit," James spits. "That's total bullshit."

"I know—I'm sorry, and—"

"No, I mean why can't you both just work here?"

Now I'm the one who goes silent. Do they actually want *me* to stay? And this is from *James?*

"Yeah, I don't see the big deal," Scott concurs.

Rocket bobs his head. "Me neither."

I rub my lips together, formulating a plan. "Well, let's go get him back. We'll drive the truck over with Elmore and demand a swap."

The guys relax into grins. "Sounds like a plan to me," Scott says. "I'll go tell the captain."

On the way over, the guys pepper me with questions. "So are you two in a fight or something? Over who leaves here?"

I keep my eyes on the road, putting my lights on when traffic sucks and we can't get through. "Sorta, yeah. It was more than that, but yeah."

"So is this gonna be the make up? Like we're all gonna witness it?" Rocket asks.

My cheeks grow warm. "Shut up. I'm not going to French kiss him in front of you or anything."

"Well I was just thinking we should go in with the big guns. Like you should buy some roses and we can set up the ladder so you can go and get him *Pretty Woman* style," Rocket says.

I laugh.

"Yes!" James says. "You have to. Captain will never live it down for the rest of his career."

"Um, wouldn't that be reason enough *not* to do it? Plus, making things public would ensure they never let us work together, no matter what," I say, even though I've already decided to go to the training Blaze signed me up for. I think his instincts for me were actually dead-on, I was just too busy being pissed to realize it.

"Yeah, that's true," Scott agrees. "Okay, no ladder and roses. We'll just go in like it's a kidnapping. We'll throw a bag over his head and wrestle him out."

"No, no, no wait," James exclaims. "First we truss Elmore up and then we offer him like a hostage exchange."

"Perfect," I agree. I glance over my shoulder and find them all smiling, including Elmore, who is offering his wrists up to be bound.

We pull up in front of their station and get out, shoving our hostage in front of us while we walk, gang-style into the open bay.

"Your captain for our captain, right now," Scott yells. "Unless you want us to throw him in the Hudson."

Chuckles greet us. Their crew saunters out, including Blaze who appears, scratching his handsome jaw. His gaze dances over me, and when I wink, a broad grin creases his face.

We pull the paper bag—all we could find—off Captain Elmore's head and I attempt to put it over Blaze's, which forces me to jump like a little kid. Fortunately, Blaze lowers down to make it easier for me, his blue-eyed gaze burning into mine, lighting a fire in my low-belly, a tingling between my legs.

His gaze promises retribution, play—so much more.

He even holds his hands out and we wrap a rubber tube—our makeshift rope—around his wrists. Then I take one of his elbows and Rocket takes the other and we escort him back to the fire truck.

Just as we get a call.

I flip on the sirens and we're off—no time to hash things out or celebrate, just the team, reunited, doing what we do: save lives and put out fires.

EPILOGUE

laze

I FINISH my preparations and do a quick pickup of my apartment before Lia arrives.

Tonight is punishment number three.

I've been trying my damnedest not to move too fast again. And failing miserably. It's been four weeks since Lia and the crew came to get me from the other station, and I've done everything I can to do this right. I've kept the kink to a minimum, let her lead.

To my delight, she did end up taking the certificate training to be a fire inspector, which is both wonderful and horrible, because she's been too busy to hang out.

But she's the one who asked me for this. Reminded me she still had a punishment coming.

She told me about her birthday—how her family already knew

she was responsible for the fire and had forgiven her. I think her guilt is mostly gone. Which means tonight is purely for play.

I think that's better, anyway. I don't want her thinking I'm trying to fix anything.

She knocks on the door and I answer it. Even though I told her what to wear and should be prepared, my dick punches out like a flag when I see her schoolgirl outfit.

"In my bedroom—panties and shoes off, but leave the rest of that cute little outfit on. Then you're going to go onto knees and forearms with your nose to the corner."

"Okay, Daddy." She flashes me a naughty smile—probably guessing she has me by the balls so hard right now.

I have to close my eyes and count to fifty to keep from following her right in. But I wait. I don't even let myself squeeze my aching cock through my jeans. I'm going to make this night good for her—memorable. I walk stiffly—because my pants are too tight—to the kitchen and grab the ginger finger floating inside a bowl of iced water.

I did a little research—surfed the spanking porn—and came upon a thing called figging. It's basically using a ginger butt plug as punishment. It causes a burning sensation in the anus, which seemed appropriate for my little pyro.

I open the door.

"Jesus *fuck*," I curse. The sight of Lia nearly drops me to my knees. I've never seen anything so flaming hot in my life. She's in the position I described, her ass lifted in the air, the navy uniform skirt flipped up on her back to give me the full view of her enticing bare ass and the sweet little pussy glistening below.

Now I can't help but squeeze my cock. "Good girl." My voice sounds scratchy. I kneel at her side and run my hand over her fine ass like it's a masterpiece—which it is. Then I add my own color to the masterpiece by smacking, hard.

She grunts but stays in position. I slap each cheek, alternating, until pink handprints show up on her caramel skin. Then I use two fingers to pry her asscheeks apart and press the tip of the ginger finger I carved into the shape of a butt plug against her anus.

She squeals and attempts to pinch her cheeks together. I keep up the pressure. "Take your punishment, Lia." I make my voice firm.

"Wh-what is it?" her voice wobbles, but I doubt it's from fear.

"Ginger. Have you ever heard of figging?"

"Did you say ginger?"

"Open, Lia. *Now*."

She relaxes and I push the ginger in. It's not particularly wide, so it goes in without lube, which I learned is important when figging.

"Good girl. Yes, I put ginger root in your ass. Girls who play with matches get their assholes set on fire."

"*Ohmygod*," she whimpers.

I reward her compliance by stroking her dewy pussy, slipping one finger inside her, then two. She moans, but I don't give her more than a couple pumps before withdrawing and circling her clit.

She whimpers again and rolls her hips back even more.

I slap her pussy and get up. "Don't move from this position, baby. I want you to stay here until your asshole's on fire and your pussy's leaking like a faucet."

"Blaze," she pants.

"You tell me when it's time. Ask for your spanking and I'll give it to you good, baby." I move to sit on the edge of the bed and take off my shoes and shirt. "And then I'll fuck you until tomorrow with that ginger still in your ass."

Lia groans and rolls her head around on the cushion I put down for her to kneel on. "You're killing me, Blaze."

"Oh I'm just warming up, little girl. Warming *you* up."

Waiting sucks. According to my research, it takes about ten minutes for the ginger to start to burn. I can hardly stand it. My situation may be more comfortable than Lia's, but I have to look at her while my jeans strangle my cock.

The first few minutes, she's still. Then she starts to shift around from knee to knee. Her anus clenches around the ginger and she lets out a groan. She whines and rubs her face on the cushion, moans some more. When the clenching of her anus and pussy grow more frequent and her whimpers more plaintive, I call her over.

"Ready for your spanking, angel?"

She stands up, smoothing her skirt. Her face is flushed, pigtails askew.

"Come lie over Daddy's lap." I pat my knee.

She comes immediately, like she knows I'm her salvation. Tips herself over my knee and wiggles her cute little ass.

I flip her skirt up and pump the ginger finger in and out of her. She moans her pleasure, her distress. I spank her. It's a good, solid spanking—hard slaps that make her jerk and twist, and I don't take it slow. I give it to her fast and hard until she's squirming right and left, whimpering and moaning for release. And then I plunge three fingers into her her wet heat, make them into a cone and fuck her with them.

Her pussy's never felt so hot, so wet, so swollen. "Blaze, please," she moans.

"You ready for my cock?"

"You have no idea," she moans, and I lose all control.

I hold her torso down while I pull my leg out from under her, so she's bent over the bed now. I twiddle the ginger in her ass with one hand while I work open the button of my jeans with the other. Then it's a rip, snap, roll to get a condom on and push against her entrance.

I sink into her easily. She's tight, but so juicy wet, so ready, her pussy seems to pull me in, welcome me. Her muscles squeeze and she moans wantonly. I interlace my fingers over the tops of hers and fuck her deep. Nothing compares to the glory of being inside her, of knowing she wants me to take her as hard and rough as I crave.

I slap my loins against her pink ass, listening to the little grunts and cries she makes.

"More," she moans. "Harder."

I slam into her harder, drive deeper. "You like it rough, don't you, baby?"

"Please," she moans. "Please, Blaze."

I unwind the fingers of my right hand from hers and insinuate it beneath her hips. One touch of her clit is all it takes.

She screams and tightens around my dick. Her orgasm rolling in, I allow myself to surrender to the pleasure, as well. In just a few more strokes, I join her, bellowing, "yes!" at the top of my lungs.

I clean up and lift her into my bed, offer her water and caresses.

She curls into me and I wrap my body around her protectively. She brings out every ounce of hero I have in me, all directed at her.

"Move in with me," I blurt before I can stop myself.

She opens her eyes, and gives me a sleepy look. "Okay."

A relieved laugh escapes my lips. "Okay? Really? I didn't ask too soon?"

"Oh, you asked way too soon, but I don't care. I'm ready to let you take care of me."

My chest squeezes so tight I can't breathe. "Yeah?" I choke out.

She rakes her fingernails over my chest, traces the lines of my tattoos. "As long as you let me rescue you, too, sometimes."

"Every day," I say gruffly. "You rescue me every fucking day I get to see you." I bring my mouth down on hers, kissing and sucking her pouty lips until I'm sure she knows who I belong to. It's her, all the way.

Only her.

The End

I HOPE YOU LOVED BLAZE! If you haven't read my sexy mafia romance **King of Diamonds,** I hope you'll check it out!

Be sure to read the other books in the *Hard n' Dirty* Series:

Getting Dirty by Aubrey Cara
Filthy Fight by Alta Hensley
Hard Wood by Tara Crescent
Blaze by Renee Rose
Hammered by Alexis Alvarez
Jacked Up by Jane Henry
Drilled by Ava Sinclair
Beauty and the Lumberjacks by Lee Savino

HAMMERED - SNEAK PEEK

Be sure to check out the next book in the Hard n' Dirty series -
Hammered by Alexis Alvarez

The environmental chick? Yeah, she's hot.

I'd love to bend her over the hood of her stupid little electric car and smack that ass.

But the project comes first.

I don't have time for dating, especially tree-huggers. I have to get this build completed on time.

But a kiss never hurt anyone... right?

She just better not be playing me to get info on my boss. Or shut down this project.

Because she'll find out that I can give as good as I get.

That I have creative ways to punish her.

Get her begging for more...

Hammered Chapter One - Preview

Talia

"No problem getting through that fence." I turn to my friend and partner in crime, Lem, and give her a bright smile. "Now we need to find the elusive Danton Carter."

Across the construction site, a few men in hard hats turn to stare. When they don't look away immediately, my heart rate accelerates.

Lem rolls her eyes and touches her skirt. "Not loving the dust, Talia."

"I don't want to get kicked out before we talk to their boss." I scan the area. "Do you see him anywhere?" I push my hair out of my face. "It's so humid."

My eyes catch on a man by a stack of 2x4s. He's tall and built, and has the beginnings of a scruffy beard on his chiseled face. Super hot. He meets my eyes and I look away quickly.

"Too bad we're not looking for that guy." Lem nods her head in his direction. "Right?"

"If it doesn't have a beer gut, several rows of jowls, and a cowboy hat with a feather, it isn't Danton Carter. Once you see his pic on the website, you can't unsee it."

"Hot guy is staring." Lem steps closer to me.

"Act like we belong. Walk that way." I point to a silver trailer. "Maybe Carter's in there, eating pork rinds."

Lem snorts.

"Actually, he's not eating pork rinds. He's devouring the small, delicate bodies of the Moorish Crane. The very ones we're trying to save. The ones he's killing with this expansion into the woods." My voice rises.

The handsome man puts down his hammer, unwraps a flannel shirt from his waist, and wipes his face with it.

Jesus, this guy is ripped! In his mid-thirties, I'd guess, his tanned skin is muscled like a fitness model, with a six-pack, strong biceps and triceps, narrow hips, and broad shoulders. His blue jeans ride low on his hips, and those boots… I do have a thing for guys in boots and worn jeans.

He tosses his shirt onto the pile of wood and strides toward me and my bestie, adjusting his hard hat.

"Talia. Incoming."

"I can see that," I hiss back, adjusting my skirt, wishing my heels weren't so high. If I had sneakers on, I'd already be banging on that trailer.

"Ladies." His voice is low and rich, but not welcoming. "This is a construction site. Private property. I need you to leave."

I stick out my hand. "Hi. I'm Talia Carlsson and this is my colleague, Lem Hayes. We're both volunteers from the—"

He doesn't take my hand. "I don't care where you're from; you need to exit the premises. You're not authorized, and you don't have hard hats and boots. Let's go."

He gestures to the fence and gate. "I assumed the *Employees Only* sign might keep random people out. And the lock." He narrows his eyes.

I cough. "It was left open."

The man smiles, but it seems sort of predatory. "I suppose if I watched the security footage, I'd see exactly how you got in."

"Maybe there's no need to do that." Lem pulls at my sleeve. "We can leave right now."

"Not until we speak to Danton Carter." I cross my arms.

The man stills. "What do you want with Danton Carter?"

"We're from Earth First Environmentals." I reach into my case and pull out a card. "My contact info."

He takes the card and slides it into his front pocket without reading it, an easy move that makes my stomach flip, as I look at his lean hips. "Let me guess." His voice is flat. "You're with the group that keeps pestering us."

"If you give us a chance to talk to him, I would appreciate it." I make eye contact to show my sincerity. His eyes are a gorgeous cerulean blue. Holy mother of everything, who has eyes like that? And those lashes?

"Ladies, we need to walk." His hand hovers just above my shoulder. "If you are injured on this site, it's my ass."

I try not to think about how much I'd like his ass, and how nice it looks in those jeans. I feel the warmth from his hand, and even though he doesn't touch me, a little shiver of arousal sparks in my core.

"We're not going near the work zone. We just wanted to find Danton." I look back. "Or someone who knows where he is. Can you tell me where to find him?"

"The dangers are not limited to being hit in the head with an I-beam. You could trip over your own feet, fall and break your neck, and then sue." He blows out a breath.

"Does that happen super often?" Lem's voice is innocent.

"When people wear shoes like that, you better damn well believe it," he says, a note of disgust in his tone, pointing at my heels.

"Ooh, no, these shoes are very comfortable," I disagree, glancing down. "I walk quite well in them."

Then I trip over an air molecule and fall right into the man.

Strong chest. Abs of steel. Arms that encircle me with strength. And his scent – not sweaty, like you'd assume, but sort of clean. Like soap, faint aftershave. Then a hint of deodorant and musk.

It's over fast, then I'm back on my feet, breathing a little hard.

"Exactly," he says, condescension dripping from his voice, "what I was talking about." He rolls his eyes at me and Lem, but mostly at me. "Are you alright?" It's like those last words were pulled from him.

"Yes." I take a breath. "I only did that"—I sniff—"to make you feel good about yourself, like you get things right sometimes. It was intentional." I stick up my chin and cross my arms. "You're welcome." I uncross my arms and adjust my hair, and his eyes follow the movement.

He scowls at me, hands on his hips, and slowly a smile works its way to his lips. "Is that so."

"It's exactly so." My mouth twitches. "Because now that you're softened up, you're going to take us to see Danton Carter. Who's one elusive... guy." *Sonofabitch*, is what I wanted to say, but probably it's not the best idea to insult a man's boss in front of him.

"If he's elusive to you, Ms."—he pulls the card from his pocket and glances at it—"Carlsson, it's for a reason. Have you considered that?"

"What's your name again?"

He quirks a brow. "Again? Don't recall I told it to you, yet."

"You didn't. That was my way of asking."

"Kind of a roundabout way, don't you think?"

"So what is it?"

He smiles at me. "You can call me Dane. Dane... Troy."

"And this"—he gestures at the fence through which we recently came—"is called the exit. And this"—he raises his hand in a little Miss America wave—"is goodbye."

"But wait."

"Nice chatting, ladies." He fixes us with a steely stare, and I gulp, stepping back through the opening with Lem. He clicks the lock shut and crosses his arms over that impressive chest. "You two have a fantastic day."

When we don't make a move to walk away, he raises one brow. "I'd sure hate to have to call security, which I will do in half a heartbeat if I see either of you two around here again in those." He waves a hand at my heels, then turns to go.

"So I can come back if I wear my combat boots?" I call, and he snorts, turns back as if he can't resist one more look.

"Please," I implore. "It's important. We have a miniscule

window of opportunity here, and we only need a few minutes of his time. I've tried all the more traditional means—"

"You mean legitimate—"

"He's not responding to emails, phone calls, texts, tweets."

"If he's not responding, it means the answer to whatever you want is probably already a no. Thank him for saving you some time," he says drily. "Bye."

Lem and I stand shoulder to shoulder, watching as he strides back to his pile of boards. He picks up the shirt and puts it on without glancing in our direction, then heads over to the group of men nearby.

"Is he a foreman?" Lem rummages in her purse and grabs her keys.

"He's a dick." I scowl.

"I'm sorry." Lem turns to me. "That did not go well."

"Understatement. Did we look stupid?"

"Well, women and feminists everywhere are crying, so I'd have to go with a resounding yes." Lem shakes her head.

I groan in frustration as we get into her Prius. "I just thought if we could see him, face to face. Once. But we can't even get past his guard dog."

"It's not over," she consoles me. "They're not scheduled to break into the breeding grounds for a few weeks, right? So you have time to track him down. Make your case."

"Yeah." I stare at the plastic banner that sways in the desultory breeze. *Danton Carter Construction Corp.* It's held up on either side by two rough pieces of wood, one of which has pink spray paint. I see more pink marks along the ground, a dashed line, probably tracing the path of a future gas line or electric wire. "They've already built this much. Why would they change it now just because we asked?"

Lem nods. "And since everything they're doing is legal, they don't need to."

"Maybe Mark is right. I'm wasting my time on this crane project."

"Well, the thing about *your* time is that only you get to decide. Although…" she trails off and glances at me.

"What?"

"I mean, there *are* other breeding grounds for the cranes. And we do have other issues to handle. I hate to say bigger ones, but…" she pauses again. "I mean, you know I agree that Mark's a douche ninety percent of the time. But he may be right, just this once."

"Please. Ninety-five, Lem. Get it right."

We both laugh, and she slows down to drive over a series of muddy bumps and a well of murky water in between.

"This is really far out. Weird place for corporate offices, don't you think?" Lem looks out at the wild tangle of bushes that leads into the woods.

"That's the thing. The zoning paperwork is so vague it could be anything." I pull up the stack of printouts from my laptop case near my feet. "We're assuming corporate offices. But maybe it's a personal retreat for the big man himself. Funded with company money."

"The legal team tried to untangle it and said it's legit, though. Right?"

"Yup. And Mark said he needs them to work the sea lion issue in Carlsbad." I sigh. "Wish I'd gone to law school sometimes."

"Buy a box of Cracker Jack." Lem snorts. "I hear they have some degrees in there."

I smile, but then frown as we pass a meadow. "I bet he plans to develop all of this into urban blight. I can't believe they sold him the land. Assholes, all of them. Our current city council sucks."

"Don't disagree there."

When we make it to the main road, gravel pings the underside of the car as Lem pulls out. "Where to now?"

"Back to the volunteer office." I scowl. "We have to figure out our next steps."

But as we drive, I can't get the image of Dane Troy out of my mind. Those eyes, those muscles. That mouth. And I can't deny that even if we didn't exactly get along, I'm dying to see him again.

Read Hammered now

WANT MORE? KING OF DIAMONDS
EXCERPT

Sondra

I tug down the hem of my one-piece, zippered housekeeping uniform dress. The Pepto Bismol pink number comes to my upper thighs and fits like a glove, hugging my curves, showing off my cleavage. Clearly, the owners of the Bellissimo Hotel and Casino want their maids to look as hot as their cocktail girls.

I went with it. I'm wearing a pair of platform-heeled wraparounds comfortable enough to clean rooms in, but sexy enough to show off the muscles in my legs, and I pulled my shoulder-length blonde hair into two fluffy pigtails.

When in Vegas, right?

My feminist friends from grad school would have a fit with this.

I push the not-so-little housekeeping cart down the hallway of the grand hotel portion of the casino. I spent all morning cleaning people's messes. And let me tell you, the messes in Vegas are big. Drug paraphernalia. Semen. Condoms. Blood. And this is an expensive, high-class place. I've only worked here two weeks and I've already seen all that and more.

I work fast. Some of the maids recommend taking your time so you don't get overloaded, but I still hope to impress someone at the Bellissimo into giving me a better job. Hence dressing like the casino version of the French maid fantasy.

Dolling myself up was probably prompted by what my cousin Corey dubs, *The Voice of Wrong.* I have the opposite of a sixth sense or voice of reason, especially when it comes to the male half of the population.

Why else would I be broke and on the rebound from the two-timing party boy I left in Reno? I'm a smart woman. I have a master's degree. I had a decent adjunct faculty position and a bright future.

But when I realized all my suspicions about Tanner cheating on me were true, I packed the Subaru I shared with him and left for Vegas to stay with Corey, who promised to get me a job dealing cards with her here.

But there aren't any dealer jobs available at the moment—only housekeeping. So now I'm at the bottom of the totem pole, broke, single, and without a set of wheels because my car got totaled in a hit and run the day I arrived.

Not that I plan to stay here long-term. I'm just testing the waters in Vegas. If I like it, I'll apply for adjunct college teaching jobs. I've even considered substitute teaching high school once I have the wheels to get around.

If I'm able to land a dealer job, though, I'll take it because the money would be three times what I'd make in the public school system. Which is a tragedy to be discussed on another day.

I head back into the main supply area which doubles as my boss' office and load up my cart in the housekeeping cave, stacking towels and soap boxes in neat rows.

"Oh for God's sake." Marissa, my supervisor, shoves her phone in the pocket of her housekeeping dress. A hot forty-two-year-old, she fills hers out in all the right places, making it look like a dress she chose to wear, rather than a uniform. "I have four people out sick today. Now I have to go do the bosses' suites myself," she groans.

I perk up. I know—that's *The Voice of Wrong*. I have a morbid fascination with everything mafioso. Like, I've watched every episode of *The Sopranos* and have memorized the script from *The Godfather*.

"You mean the Tacones' rooms? I'll do them." It's stupid, but I want a glimpse of them. What do real mafia men look like? Al Pacino? James Gandolfini? Or are they just ordinary guys? Maybe I've already passed them while pushing my cart around.

"I wish, but you can't. It's a special security clearance thing. And believe me—you don't want to. They are super paranoid and picky as hell. You can't look at the wrong thing without getting ripped a new one. They definitely wouldn't want to see anyone new up there. I'd probably lose my job over it, as a matter of fact."

I should be daunted, but this news only adds to the mystique I created in my mind around these men. "Well, I'm willing and available, if you want me to. I already finished my hallway. Or I could go with you and help? Make it go faster?"

I see my suggestion worming through her objections. Interest flits over her face, followed by more consternation.

I adopt a hopeful-helpful expression.

"Well, maybe that would be all right...I'd be supervising you, after all."

Yes! I'm dying of curiosity to see the mafia bosses up close. Foolish, I know, but I can't help it. I want to text Corey to tell her the news, but there isn't time. Corey knows all about my fascination, since I already pumped her for information.

Marissa loads a few other things on my cart and we head off

together for the special bank of elevators—the only ones that go all the way to the top of the building and require a keycard to access.

"So, these guys are really touchy. Most times they're not in their rooms, and then all you have to worry about is staying away from their office desks," Marissa explains once we left the last public floor and it was just the two of us in the elevator. "Don't open any drawers—don't do anything that appears nosy. I'm serious—these guys are scary."

The doors swish open and I push the cart out, following her around the bend to the first door. The sound of loud, male voices comes from the room.

Marissa winces. *"Always knock,"* she whispers before lifting her knuckles to rap on the door.

They clearly don't hear her, because the loud talking continues.

She knocks again and the talking stops.

"Yeah?" a deep masculine voice calls out.

"Housekeeping."

We wait as silence greets her call. After a moment the door swings open to reveal a middle-aged guy with slightly graying hair. "Yeah, we were just leaving." He pulls on what must be a thousand dollar suit jacket. A slight gut thickens his middle, but otherwise he's extremely good-looking. Behind him stand three other men, all dressed in equally nice suits, none wearing their jackets.

They ignore us as they push past, resuming their conversation in the hallway. "So I tell him…" The door closes behind them.

"Whew," Marissa breathes. "It's way easier if they're not here." She glances up at the corners of the rooms. "Of course there are cameras everywhere, so it's not like we aren't being watched." She points to a tiny red light shining from a little device mounted at the juncture of the wall and ceiling. I've already noticed them all over the casino. "But it's less nerve-wracking if we're not tiptoeing around them."

She jerks her head down the hall. "You take the bathroom and bedrooms, I'll do the kitchen, office and living area."

"Got it." I grab the supplies I need off the cart and head in the direction she indicated.

The bedroom's well-appointed in a nondescript way. I pull the sheets and bedspread up to make the bed. The sheets were probably 3,000 thread count, if there is such a thing. That may be an exaggeration but, really, they are amazing.

Just for kicks, I rub one against my cheek.

It's so smooth and soft. I can't imagine what it would be like to lie in that bed. I wonder which of the guys slept in here. I make the bed with hospital corners, the way Marissa trained me to, dust and vacuum, then move on to the second bedroom and then the bathroom. When I finish, I find Marissa vacuuming in the living room.

She switches it off and winds up the cord. "All done? Me too. Let's go to the next one."

I push out the cart and she taps on the door of the suite down the hall. No answer.

She keys us in. "It is way faster having you help," she says gratefully.

I flash her a smile. "I think it's more fun to work as a team, too."

She smiles back. "Yeah, somehow I don't think they would go for it as a regular thing, but it's nice for a change."

"Same routine?"

"Unless you want to switch? This one only has one bedroom."

"Nah," I say, "I like bed/bath." Of course that's because of my all-consuming curiosity. There are more personal effects in a bedroom and a bathroom, not that I saw anything of interest in the last place. I didn't go poking around, of course. The cameras in every corner have me nervous.

This place is the same as the last, as if they'd paid a decorator to furnish them and they were all identical. High luxury, but not much personality. Well, from what I understand, the Tacone family—at least the ones who run the Bellissimo—are all single men. What can I expect?

I make the bed and move on to dusting.

From the living room, I hear Marissa's voice.

"What?" I call out, but then I realize she's talking on the phone.

She comes in a moment later, breathless. "I have to go." Her face has gone pale. "My kid's been taken to the ER for a concussion."

"Oh shit. Go—I've got this. Do you want to give me the keycard for the last suite?" There are three suites on this top floor.

She looks around distractedly. "No, I'd better not. Could you just finish this place up and head back downstairs? I'll call Samuel to let him know what happened." Samuel's our boss, the head of housekeeping. "Don't forget to stay away from the desk in the office."

"Sure thing. Get out of here." I make a shooing motion. "Go be with your kid."

"Okay." She digs her purse out from the cart and slings it over her shoulder. "I'll see you tomorrow."

"I hope he's all right," I say to her back as she leaves.

She flings a weak smile over her shoulder. "Thanks. Bye."

I grab the vacuum and head back into the bedroom. When I finish, I hear male voices in the living room.

"Hope you can get some sleep, Nico. How long's it been?" one of the voices asked.

"Forty-eight hours. Fucking insomnia."

"G'luck, see you later." A door clicks shut.

My heart immediately beats a little faster with excitement or nerves. Yes—I'm a fool. Later, I would realize my mistake in not marching right out and introducing myself, but Marissa has me nervous about the Tacones and I freeze up. The cart stands out in the living room, though. I decide to go into the bathroom and clean everything I can without getting fresh supplies. Finally, I give up, square my shoulders and head out.

I arrive in the living room and pull out three folded towels, four hand towels and four washcloths. Out of my peripheral vision, I watch the broad shoulders and back of another finely dressed man.

He glances over then does a double-take. His dark eyes rake over me, lingering on my legs and traveling up to my breasts, then face. *"Who the fuck are you?"*

I should've expected that response, but it startles me anyway. He sounds scary. Seriously scary, and he walks toward me like he means business. He's beautiful, with dark wavy hair, a stubbled square jaw and thick-lashed eyes that bore a hole right through me.

"Huh? Who. The fuck. Are you?"

I panic. Instead of answering him, I turn and walk swiftly to the bathroom, as if putting fresh towels in his bathroom will fix everything.

He stalks after me and follows me in. "What are you doing in here?" He knocks the towels out of my hands.

Stunned, I stare down at them scattered on the floor. "I'm...housekeeping," I offer lamely. Damn my idiotic fascination with the mafia. This is not the freaking *Sopranos*. This is a real-life, dangerous man wearing a gun in a holster under his armpit. I know, because I see it when he reaches for me.

He grips my upper arms. "Bullshit. No one who looks like"—his eyes travel up and down the length of my body again—*"you—* works in housekeeping."

I blink, not sure what that means. I'm pretty, I know that, but there's nothing special about me. I'm your girl-next-door blue-eyed blonde type, on the short and curvy side. Not like my cousin Corey, who is tall, slender, red-haired and drop-dead gorgeous, with the confidence to match.

There's something lewd in the way he looks at me that makes it sound like I'm standing there in nipple tassels and a G-string instead of my short, fitted maid's dress. I play dumb. "I'm new. I've only been here a couple weeks."

He sports dark circles under his eyes, and I remember what he told the other man. He suffers from insomnia. Hasn't slept in forty-eight hours.

"Are you bugging the place?" he demands.

"Wha—" I can't even answer. I just stare like an idiot.

He starts frisking me for a weapon. "Is this a con? What do they think—I'm going to fuck you? Who sent you?"

I attempt to answer, but his warm hands sliding all over me make me forget what I was going to say. *Why is he talking about fucking me?*

He stands up and gives me a tiny shake. "Who. Sent. You?" His dark eyes mesmerize. He smells of the casino—of whiskey and cash, and beneath it, his own simmering essence.

"No one...I mean, Marissa!" I exclaim her name like a secret password, but it only seems to irritate him further.

He reaches out and runs his fingers swiftly along the collar of my housekeeping dress, as if checking for some hidden wiretap. I'm pretty sure the guy's half out of his mind, maybe delirious with sleep deprivation. Maybe just nuts. I freeze, not wanting to set him off.

To my shock, he yanks down the zipper on the front of my dress, all the way to my waist.

If I were my cousin Corey, daughter of a mean FBI agent, I'd knee him in the balls, gun or not. But I was raised not to make waves. To be a nice girl and do what authority tells me to do.

So, like a freaking idiot, I just stand there. A tiny mewl leaves my lips, but I don't dare move, don't protest. He yanks the form-fitting dress to my waist and jerks it down over my hips.

I wrest my arms free from the fabric to wrap them around myself.

Nico Tacone shoves me aside to get the dress out from under my feet. He picks it up and runs his hands all over it, still searching for the mythical wiretap while I shiver in my bra and panties.

I fold my arms across my breasts. "Look, I'm not wearing a wire or bugging the place," I breathe. "I was helping Marissa and then she got a call—"

"Save it," he barks. "You're too fucking perfect. What's the con? What the fuck are you doing in here?"

I'm confounded. Should I keep arguing the truth when it only pisses him off? I swallow. None of the words in my head seem like the right ones to say.

He reaches for my bra.

I bat at his hands, heart pumping like I just did two back-to-back spin classes. He ignores my feeble resistance. The bra is a front hook and he obviously excels at removing women's lingerie because it's off faster than the dress. My breasts spring out with a bounce, and he glares at them, as if I bared them just to tempt him. He examines the bra, then tosses it on the floor and stares at me. His eyes dip once more to my breasts and his expression grows even more furious. "Real tits," he mutters as if that's a punishable offense.

I try to step back but I bump into the toilet. "I'm not hiding anything. I'm just a maid. I got hired two weeks ago. You can call Samuel."

He steps closer. Tragically, the hardened menace on his handsome face only increases his attractiveness to me. I really am wired wrong. My body thrills at the nearness of him, pussy dampening. Or maybe it's the fact that he just stripped me practically naked while he stands there fully clothed. I think this is a fetish to some people. Apparently, I'm one of them. If I wasn't so scared, it would be uber hot.

He palms my backside, warm fingers sliding over the satiny fabric of my panties, but he's not groping me, he's still working efficiently, checking for bugs. He slides a thumb under the gusset, running the fabric through his fingers. My belly flutters.

Oh God. The back of his thumb brushes my dewy slit. I cringe in embarrassment. His head jerks up and he stares at me in surprise, nostrils flaring.

Then his brows slammed down as if it pisses him off I'm turned on, as if it's a trick.

That's when things really go to shit.

He pulls out his gun and points it at my head—actually pushes the cold hard muzzle against my brow. "*What. The fuck. Are you doing here?*"

I pee myself.

Literally.

God help me.

I freeze and pee trickles down my inner thighs before I can stop it. My face burns with humiliation.

Now, the anger and indignation I should've had from the start rushes out. It's the exact wrong moment to get lippy, but I glare at him. "What's *wrong* with you?"

He stares at the dribble on the floor. I think he's going to... Well, I don't know what I think he'll do—pistol whip me or sneer or something—but his expression relaxes and he shoves the gun in its holster. Apparently, I finally gave the right reaction.

He grips my arm and drags me toward the shower. My brain is doing flip flops trying to get back online. To figure out what in the hell is happening and how I can get myself out of this very crazy, very fucked up situation.

Tacone reaches in and turns on the water, holding his hand under the spray as if to check its temperature.

My brain hasn't turned back on, but I wrestle with his grip on my arm.

He releases it and holds his palm face out. "Okay," he says. "Get in." He draws his hand out of the shower and jerks his head toward the spray. "Clean up."

Is he coming in there with me? Or is this really just about washing off?

Fuck it. I *am* a mess. I kick off my shoes and step in, panties and all.

I don't know how long I stand there, drowning in shock. After a while, I blink and awareness seeps back in. Then I freak out. What in the hell is happening? What will he do with me? Did I really just pee on his floor? I want to die of embarrassment.

Keep it together, Sondra.

Jesus Christ. The mafia boss who stands on the other side of the shower curtain thinks I'm a narc. Or a spy or rat—whatever they call it. And he just stripped me down to my panties and pointed a gun at my head. Things could only get worse from here. A sob rises up in my throat.

Don't cry. Not a good time to cry.

I stumble back against the tile wall, my legs too rubbery to stand. Hot tears spill down my cheeks and I sniff.

The shower curtain peeps open right by my face and I jerk back. I didn't know he was standing right outside it.

Read now (free in Kindle Unlimited)

WANT FREE RENEE ROSE BOOKS?

Click here to sign up for Renee Rose's newsletter and receive a free copy of *Theirs to Protect, Owned by the Marine, Theirs to Punish, The Alpha's Punishment, Disobedience at the Dressmaker's* and *Her Billionaire Boss*. In addition to the free stories, you will also get special pricing, exclusive previews and news of new releases.

ABOUT RENEE ROSE

USA TODAY BESTSELLING AUTHOR RENEE ROSE is a naughty wordsmith who writes kinky romance novels. Named Eroticon USA's Next Top Erotic Author in 2013, she has also won *Spunky and Sassy's* Favorite Sci-Fi and Anthology Author, *The Romance Reviews* Best Historical Romance, and *Spanking Romance Reviews'* Best Historical, Best Erotic, Best Ageplay and favorite author. She's hit #1 on Amazon in the Erotic Paranormal, Western and Sci-fi categories. She also pens BDSM stories under the name Darling Adams.

Please follow her on:
  Bookbub | Goodreads | Instagram

Renee loves to connect with readers!
www.reneeroseromance.com
reneeroseauthor@gmail.com

Paranormal

Bad Boy Alphas Series

Alpha's Mission

Alpha's War

Alpha's Desire

Alpha's Obsession

Alpha's Challenge

Alpha's Prize

Alpha's Danger

Alpha's Temptation

Love in the Elevator (Bonus story to Alpha's Temptation)

Alpha Doms Series

The Alpha's Hunger

The Alpha's Promise

The Alpha's Punishment

Other Paranormals

His Captive Mortal

Deathless Love

Deathless Discipline

The Winter Storm: An Ever After Chronicle

Sci-Fi

Zandian Masters Series

His Human Slave

His Human Prisoner

Training His Human

His Human Rebel

His Human Vessel

His Mate and Master

Zandian Pet

Their Zandian Mate

His Human Possession

Zandian Brides (Reverse Harem)

Night of the Zandians

Bought by the Zandians

The Hand of Vengeance

Her Alien Masters

Regency

The Darlington Incident

Humbled

The Reddington Scandal

The Westerfield Affair

Pleasing the Colonel

Western

His Little Lapis

The Devil of Whiskey Row

The Outlaw's Bride

Medieval

Mercenary

Medieval Discipline

Lords and Ladies

The Knight's Prisoner

Betrothed

Held for Ransom

The Knight's Seduction

The Conquered Brides (5 book box set)

Renaissance

Renaissance Discipline

Ageplay

Stepbrother's Rules

Her Hollywood Daddy

His Little Lapis

Black Light: Valentine's Roulette (Broken)

BDSM under the name Darling Adams
Medical Play

Yes, Doctor

Master/Slave

Punishing Portia

Made in the USA
San Bernardino, CA
01 November 2018